EMPTY EYES
A NOVEL
By
T. M. Bilderback

Copyright 2014 by T. M. Bilderback

Connect With The Author
Other Works By T. M. Bilderback

Chapter 1

I cannot express the deep, incapacitating horror and loss of hope that I feel right now. The situation in which I find myself is terribly troubling, and may spell the end...perhaps not the end of humanity, but the end of all things normal.

I'm sorry; I'm beginning this story at the end. Let me start over.

I don't know when it all started, but I know when I encountered the first signs. I was at home on a Saturday morning in September, mowing my lawn. We have no gated community, nor do we have a homeowner's association. It's a good thing, too, because they wouldn't like me very much. I don't worry about keeping my grass a quarter inch high, and I don't make "stripes" in the lawn when I mow it. I just wait until it's shaggy, then I cut it back a little to make it fairly presentable.

My neighbor, Ralph Johnson, is just the opposite. Ralph obsesses over his lawn. Crabgrass is nonexistent on his lawn, and daffodils don't dare to spawn new bulbs anywhere except a flower bed. I've actually seen Ralph on his hands and knees, ruler in hand, measuring his front lawn. He spends hours each Saturday with a lawn mower, a weed eater, and a pair of pruning shears. I've never seen anyone else as concerned over his lawn.

Ralph and his wife live on the corner of Maple and Oak. My family lives next door to them, on Maple Avenue.

We are not close.

Ralph and I have had "discussions" over my lawn care habits that have reduced themselves to carefully crafted witty insults regarding everything lawn related, including the one I zinged him with concerning going back and fertilizing his own lawn with the bullshit he was spitting out.

After that, Phyllis, my wife, and Catherine, Ralph's wife remained friendly, but Ralph and I didn't have much use for each other.

Then, the day came when one of our kids – Ralph and Catherine are childless – accidentally knocked over part of the back yard fence that separated our back lawns. It was a big, wooden, privacy fence, eight feet tall, with those pointed partial triangles at the top to discourage invaders from climbing over the top. Catherine screamed at the children, Phyl apologized. Catherine screamed at Phyl, and that was that. Ralph and I met at the broken fence that evening, I said I would happily pay to have the fence repaired, and that was that. Phyl and Catherine were no longer friendly.

Our kids, Keith and Clarissa, are still preteens. Keith is eleven, and Clarissa is twelve. Both are athletic, and, while I encourage that in them, I don't know where it comes from. I'm not athletic. Since I'm a writer, the most exercise that I get is walking a couple of blocks, mostly when I'm trying to work out a plot point. Phyllis is an accountant, and works for a major accounting firm downtown. Both of our jobs require our butts to be firmly planted in our desk chairs for extended periods. So, while we both have great metabolisms so that we don't gain weight, we don't get to do much in the way of athletics.

After I had assured Ralph that I would pay for the fence, I pulled the kids aside and told them to be more careful in the back yard. Football should not be played unless all parties make sure that nothing crashes into the fence. After that day, we didn't see much of our next-door neighbors.

So, I was very surprised that day, when I looked up from my mowing and saw Ralph walking across my front yard. He wasn't walking in a straight line, however...he would weave a couple of steps to the left, straighten up his gait, then weave a couple of steps to the right, and straighten up again. Lather, rinse, repeat. At first, I thought he had consumed one beer too many. I turned off my push mower, and waited for the man to get across the yard to me.

As he got closer, I noticed his eyes. His empty, milky eyes. They looked like light blue marbles surrounded by milk, with some red streaks in them. But, the biggest thing that I noticed about them was the fact that it seemed that he didn't really see me.

I mean, he could *see* me, obviously – the man was walking somewhat directly toward me. But he wasn't *seeing* me, if that makes any sense.

Ralph stopped two steps away, which placed him about one step away from the push mower.

Ralph, normally a fairly natty man, was dressed a bit sloppily today. Not to say that he was sloppy that day, just out of the ordinary for him. H wore a brown T-shirt, denim jeans, and tennis shoes. But he didn't have his shirttail tucked in like he normally would have, and he did not have on any socks. His hair was slightly askew, as if he had just gotten out of bed, and his glasses were crooked.

"Hello, Ralph," I said cordially.

Ralph stood looking at me with those damned empty eyes.

I decided to goad him a little bit.

"Am I mowing too loud for you? It's this new lawn mower. I don't even think it cuts evenly from the left side to the right. What do you think?"

Ralph didn't answer. He just kept looking at me.

"Ralph, is something wrong? What do you want?"

His lips began moving, but were making no sound.

"Speak up, neighbor. I can't hear you unless you make sounds."

Ralph said, "Glrk-k-k." Then he bent over at the waist and vomited about a gallon of blood all over my new Cub Cadet.

I scooted backwards quickly to avoid getting any of it on me, and I was saying, "OhmyGod! OhmyGod!"

Ralph heaved again, and vomited another gallon of blood onto my lawn mower.

But it wasn't just blood.

There was some kind of black...*ichor*...mixed in with it, in big lumps, along with squiggly, squirming things that weren't maggots, and they weren't worms. I don't know what they were, but they had legs, and scurried around the lawn mower's surface. Direct sunlight seemed to kill them, but I wasn't going to touch one to find out. The smell was horrible, and smelled as if something had died, and was rotting merrily away in the sun.

I pulled my phone out of my pocket, promptly dropped it, then picked it up and brought it out of "sleep" mode. I dialed nine-one-one, told them the emergency, and stayed on the line until the first police car arrived.

Ralph had keeled over onto his left side and pulled into a fetal position. One of those squirming things had begun to creep out of Ralph's nostril, but pulled back inside when it got close to the sunlight. His mouth was still moving, as if to form words, but the thoughts, if there were any, did not translate themselves into sound.

The cops in the squad car killed the siren, but left the lights flashing. I was on the phone with their dispatcher, told the woman that the first patrol car had arrived, and motioned the two uniformed keepers of the peace over to me.

"Are you Mr. Stiles? Mr. Paul Stiles?" asked the older cop.

"I am, and I sure am glad to see you guys!"

The younger cop squatted down beside Ralph, then reached toward Ralph's neck, presumably to check for a pulse.

"I wouldn't do that!" I said quickly. "I wouldn't touch him if I were you...at least, not bare handed. I don't believe we should touch him at all."

"Why is that, Mr. Stiles?" the cop asked.

By now, some of the neighbors had come outside to see what the fuss was about. Another siren, hopefully of an ambulance, could be heard in the distance, growing louder by the second.

I pointed to the top of the lawn mower. "I'm not sure if any of them are still alive, but those wormy-looking things with legs came out from inside Ralph when he vomited, and I saw one begin to come out of his nostril, then duck back in. You might get infected with whatever he has. I don't fancy having a bunch of...things...inside me, but you make your own mind up." I watched as the young cop drew his hand back as if it had been bitten. "Sunlight seems to kill them, though," I told him.

The siren, which did indeed belong to an ambulance, silenced as the rescue vehicle turned onto Maple from Oak. The young cop scurried away toward the new vehicle to explain what was going on. The older cop turned to me again.

"Can you tell me who this man is, Mr. Stiles?" he asked.

"Sure. He's my next door neighbor, Ralph Johnson." I pointed to the house, partially visible over the hedge on the property line. "He lives there, with his wife, Catherine." Realization dawned on me. Someone had to go tell Catherine. I didn't know who would do it, but I knew it wasn't going to be me.

"I'll go check on her, sir, and let her know what's happening. Do you know if she's home?"

I shook my head. "No idea, Officer."

His face grim, he nodded to me. "I'll go check on the wife. Please stay outside. We may have questions, and you'll need to sign a statement."

The paramedics were donning latex gloves and grabbing a stretcher from inside the ambulance. I watched them as I nodded to the cop. "Sure."

The paramedics put the stretcher down on the sidewalk in front of my house and went back to the back of their ambulance. They pulled out some bright orange plastic coveralls and pulled them on over their uniforms. The older cop had just reached the sidewalk and turned to the other side of the privacy hedge.

If Ralph had been coherent and ambulant, he probably would have screamed at the cop for "ruining his lawn". Then, he would have yelled something about the cop having no business "tearing up a good citizen's hard work". The cop probably would have shot Ralph at that point.

But, Ralph wasn't coherent or ambulant. I couldn't tell if he was even alive right now, and I sure as shit wasn't going to get any closer to him to find out.

I glanced again at the paramedics, and they had also put on those big all-over helmets with the windshield in front. Hazmat suits, I guess they were. They strapped on belts that had medium boxes attached. The boxes had hoses that connected to the backs of their helmets.

What the hell were they afraid of catching from good ol' Ralph?

Another patrol car joined the emergency vehicle parking lot in the middle of Maple. I lamented that it was still daylight. The flashing red, white, and blue lights would have been fun to watch, and very patriotic with their brightness.

The younger cop spoke with the two cops in the new patrol car, then all three cops turned toward Ralph's house. The two new cops walked onto Ralph's lawn – more "ruining" – and the younger cop stayed close to the ambulance.

Finally, the paramedics walked across my front lawn, carrying the stretcher. They stopped beside Ralph's unmoving body, and one of them turned to me.

"Mr. Stiles, did any of the vomitus touch you in any way?" asked the paramedic. His voice sounded tinny and unreal. It was coming through a small speaker near the helmet's window.

I shook my head. "No, I was able to dodge away from it. Thank God."

The paramedic's helmet nodded back and forth in an exaggerated affirmative nod. "God must have been with you today, for sure."

His partner had squatted beside Ralph. His voice sounded just as tinny and unreal as his partner's. "Looks like number twelve, Jim."

"Wow," said the paramedic referred to as "Jim". "What the hell is going on?"

"That's what I was about to ask you," I said.

The younger cop had come up to the paramedics. "Excuse me, guys, they need you next door when you get a chance."

"Next door?" I asked. "Catherine? Is she hurt?"

The young cop looked frightened and distracted as he nodded. "It looks like the same thing as with this man on the ground. They wanted me to ask you if you'd come identify her."

"Of course," I replied.

"We'll take care of your neighbor while you're over there, Mr. Stiles," said the standing paramedic.

"Thank you," I said. I walked to the end of my yard and around the hedge, into Ralph Johnson's yard. The front door was wide open.

I was alone. The younger cop had hung back with the paramedics, whether from fear, or a chance to assist them.

Ralph's lawn was immaculate. The shrubberies along the front of the house lived in beds of wood mulch, sharing their space with trimmed, blooming rose bushes, and bright, green tulips, whose blooms had already blossomed for the year. All were precisely laid out, with even spaces between each plant. Railroad ties delineated the beds, and kept the green lawn grass from intruding on the wood mulch. Decorative wrought-iron handrails decorated the sides of the steps, and met their counterparts at the top, whose job it was to keep the front porch fenced in and safely protected from those that might intrude on the privacy of the residents.

I found that I actually did feel like an intruder as I climbed those steps to the front door. With each step, a sense of dread grew stronger in me, and almost caused me to turn tail and run back to my own house, and hide safely under the king-size bed that I shared with Phyllis. I didn't, much to my later regret. I went to the open door, and spoke up.

"Hello!" I called.

"In the kitchen!" was the answer I received back.

I walked into the foyer, then down the hall to the brightly painted kitchen. The walls were painted with a bright, sunshiny yellow. The appliances were all stainless steel, shiny and spotless. The cabinets were painted with a white gloss, and the floor was white tile. The kitchen was clean and inviting, with one exception.

Catherine Johnson was curled into a fetal position on the floor, lying in a puddle of blood and black ichor. The smell of rot was present here, too. Several of the squirmy things were on the floor, but these particular squirmy things weren't dead. Sunlight hadn't touched them, and they were mindlessly scurrying around the kitchen floor. They had not left the fluid of blood and ichor...yet. They were all about three inches long, and looked like centipedes with only six legs. A single antenna waved from the front of each creature.

Catherine was dead, of that I was sure. She had a squirmy hanging from her nostril, and one peeked out from the inside of her ear.

I was glad that I had not had my lunch yet, because I wanted to finish my lawn chores first.

"Mr. Stiles, is this your neighbor?" asked the older cop.

I nodded, fighting not to retch. "Yes, officer, that's Catherine Johnson. Her husband, Ralph, is on my front lawn."

"Looks like the same thing that came over her husband," the cop said.

I was looking around the floor at the splatters of blood and ichor. There was an obvious footprint in the pool.

Someone had stepped in it.

As I watched, one of the two new cops stepped on one of the squirmy things. It splattered its insides out onto the floor and into the puddle. The other creatures came over to the crushed creature and began devouring it.

Obviously, this cop was the source of the first footprint. He probably had done the same thing.

Right after that thought came to my mind, the cop – his name plate read "Richards" – said, "Man, they sure do go after themselves, don't they?" He had a dorky, sadistic grin on his face.

The older cop's name plate read "Barnes", and the third cop's plate read "Mitchell".

Barnes looked at Richards and said, "The ME is going to be all over you for ruining evidence."

"So what?" said Richards. "The bugs killed her. Any idiot can see that!"

"But the ME doesn't need 'any idiot' ruining the evidence that shows that. Don't do it again."

I was looking at the floor while they were sorting that out, watching the squirmers. One was making its way out of the pool toward Richards' shoe. It moved quickly, and had scrabbled its way onto the top of his shoe while I opened my mouth to speak.

"Hey, Richards, you have a...," I started.

"*OW!*" shouted Richards, lifting that foot quickly and pulling up his pants leg. A small red spot was there. No squirmer. Just the spot, which looked suspiciously like a hole that wasn't bleeding.

"What's wrong with you?" asked Mitchell.

"Some fuckin' thing just bit me!" yelled Richards.

Barnes, however, was looking at me. "What did you start to say, Mr. Stiles?"

"I saw one of the squirmers work its way over to Richards' shoe. It ducked under his pants leg," I said.

"No fuckin' way!" said Richards harshly.

"Then what's that hole on your shin? Cut yourself shaving?" asked Mitchell.

"No, it just...it's only...I...," stammered Richards.

"Damn! Grab his arm, Mitchell! Let's get him to the ambulance!" shouted Barnes. "Stiles! Get out of here! Go home! Go home *now!*"

I just want you to know, there was no shame in what I did.

I ran like I never ran before.

Chapter 2

As I reached the hedge, the young cop was standing there, looking indecisive. He put his hand on his gun and said to me, "Hey! Stop! Stop right there!" He began fumbling with his holster strap when Barnes yelled from the front porch steps of Ralph's house. I stopped anyway. I didn't want to be shot by some nervous cop.

"Let him go, Tim! I told him to run!"

Tim looked at the three cops hustling across Ralph's front yard.

"Call for another ambulance, Tim! We need another ambulance! Now!"

The young cop, Tim, turned and ran to the first squad car that had arrived, and began calling his dispatcher for another ambulance. The paramedics were just loading the stretcher, which held Ralph inside of a black body bag, into the back of the ambulance, and they were still wearing their Hazmat suits. Barnes and Mitchell were literally dragging Richards to the ambulance.

"Hey! *Hey!*" yelled Barnes. One of the Hazmats turned around. Barnes said, "This man has been bitten by one of the creatures! Get him to the hospital right away! There isn't much time!"

Richards was protesting as the four men forced him into the ambulance. "No, wait, guys! You *know* me! It's *Richards*, man, come on! Nothing's wrong with me!"

In the most chilling thing I had seen so far, not because of the act, but because of the *implications* of the act, Barnes used his handcuffs to attach both of Richards hands to a handrail inside the ambulance. "Now, *go!*" shouted Barnes, as he shut the doors on Richards protests. He banged twice on the closed door. The driver climbed inside without taking off his Hazmat suit, and the ambulance pulled away with lights flashing and siren wailing.

Something occurred to me as I watched the ambulance pull away, and I turned to Barnes. "Officer Barnes...," I said.

"Sergeant, Mr. Stiles."

I shrugged. "*Sergeant* Barnes, then. I have a question."

Barnes looked around at the neighbors gathered in the street, and called out to Tim and Mitchell. "You two put some tape around these two houses, and get those people back on the sidewalks away from here! Go!" The other two cops hurried off to do what Barnes had told them.

"Okay, Stiles, looks like we have a minute to ourselves. What's your question?"

"When you left to check on Catherine, one of the paramedics said, 'Looks like number twelve.' What did he mean by that?"

Barnes took a breath like he was about to tell me to mind my own business, but something in my eyes must have changed his mind. I followed up on my question.

"Something else, too. You were awfully quick to hustle Richards off to the hospital. I think you know something you're not sharing. I'd like to know what it is," I finished.

Barnes was silent as he looked out at my neighbors. Then he looked at the two cops herding them all back away from my house and Ralph's.

Finally, Barnes turned to look at me. "Mr. Stiles...," he started.

"Paul," I interrupted.

Barnes smiled grimly at me. "Paul. My name is Bobby. And you can thank God tonight that you weren't infected. We've had calls all over the city."

"What are those things?"

Bobby shook his head. "Nobody knows. They're nothing anyone has seen before. We aren't sure where they came from, and we don't know how to kill them all." He snorted derisively. "We can't even tell when people are infected. Not until they have those empty eyes."

I started. That was the first thing I had noticed with Ralph, and I said so.

Bobby nodded. "Yeah, but your neighbor was in the last stages. The empty eyes show up about three hours before they vomit out everything. Even then, the bodies carry the eggs inside. The eggs are the black...*goo*, I guess...that comes up with the blood."

"The squirmers that Ralph hurled out all seemed to die in the sunlight."

"They aren't dead."

I looked at Bobby. "Say what?"

Bobby shook his head. "Those things aren't dead. Sunlight doesn't kill them. It only stuns them...makes them go dormant."

"Dear God. Who knows about this, Bobby? What's being done?"

"I know that three professors from the city's university are all locked up tight in their quarantine area. They're working on the problem, but they aren't coming outside. They have plenty of food and water in there, and they're making sure that nothing gets to them. One professor each of biology, physics, and chemistry. They each have an assistant inside with them, and that's it. I don't know what they've learned, and I don't know who's been told."

"Somebody needs to alert the CDC in Atlanta! Warn the Feds! Get it on the news channels! Bobby, we've got to warn people!"

"Warn them against what? We don't even know how these things spread! Richards was the first one we'd seen that had a creature infect with direct entry, but the rest of the infected people are a complete mystery! We don't know if the eggs are spread on the wind, or through the water, or just by walking on the ground."

"But people still need to be warned! Maybe they can protect themselves somehow."

Bobby looked at me. "Paul, be real. People would simply panic. They'd begin killing each other off from simple fear." He looked around at the line of neighbors again. "You married, Paul?"

I nodded. "Yeah, with two kids."

"They inside?"

"No, the kids are at the movies, and my wife is doing some work at her office downtown."

"Want some advice?"

"Sure."

Bobby looked around again. "Round 'em up, pack 'em up, and get them the hell out of here. Go somewhere far away from everyone. Protect yourself and your family." He started to walk away, then stopped and turned back to me. "But don't wait too long. Go before you can't."

I carefully considered his advice. And, on the spur of the moment, I made a decision.

"Bobby!"

He stopped walking, and turned back to me.

"Do you have a pad and pen I could use for a moment?"

"Okay." He dug in his pockets and pulled out both items, then handed them to me.

I took them, and scribbled an address, and some rudimentary directions.

"Are you married, Bobby?"

He shook his head. "Divorced."

I handed him his pad and pen. "This is the location of the cabin we own in the mountains. That's where we'll be. If it gets really bad, come there. We'd be glad to have you."

The man actually smiled. "Thanks, Paul. I may take you up on that."

I nodded at him, pulled out my cell phone, and called Phyllis as I walked toward the house.

PHYLLIS WAS FULL OF questions after I explained the day's happenings. For most of her questions, I had no answer to give her.

"So, based on what this cop said, we're going to pack up and leave town," she said, with a slightly derisive tone.

"Yes," I replied. "For a few days, at least."

"Do you have any idea how much work I have to do? It's not tax season, but it's earnings season, and some of our companies are demanding...," she started, then paused. "Paul, one of the kids is calling me. Hold on." She put me on hold.

I was thinking of ways to convince her that we had to go when she finally came back on the line.

"Paul, start packing. Let's take both the SUV and the car. We can take more with us that way."

"What happened, Phyllis? Are the kids okay?"

"That was Keith. The kids are fine, but they said that three people in the theater threw up, and ambulances carried them away. Keith is trying to be brave, but it's only for Clarissa's sake. They're scared."

"Okay, I'll get started. We need to stop by the supermarket on the way to the cabin. We have to take as much as we can, and keep clothes to a bare minimum. We can wash clothes, but food will be at a premium."

"You're right, Paul. I'll leave a note on Browning's door, just in case he doesn't answer the phone. I'll let him know that I have to take a leave of absence, and that I don't know how long I'll be. Then, I'll go get the kids and come straight home."

"Okay, Phyl. Be careful, honey. I love you."

"I love you, too, Paul."

We disconnected, and I went to the garage to dig out the suitcases.

I noticed that the Cub Cadet was still standing guard in the front yard, offering a sober reminder that my next door neighbor had just died there.

BY THE TIME PHYLLIS got home, most of the crowd had gone. The ambulance had come and gone next door, and the Johnsons' house had been sealed. The yellow tape had been moved so that my driveway wasn't blocked by it, but a square of tape surrounded the Cub Cadet. The fence of tape was four feet long on each side, and had been erected by using leftover wooden pickets from another neighbor's fence.

I went outside to meet them, mostly to keep the kids from getting too close to the lawn mower. I hugged and kissed each one, then hugged my wife fiercely.

I got the rundown about the people throwing up in the theater from Keith. He said that while no one had thrown up in their movie, they had heard about it from people that had seen it in their own movies. Since the average movie lasts two hours or less, that meant that those people had moved through to the final stage faster than Bobby had estimated to me, because no one had noticed anything about the infected people's eyes.

I warned the children not to go near the lawn mower, and began discussing how best to load the SUV with Phyllis. Suddenly, Clarissa cried out.

"Mom! Dad! There's something under the lawn mower!" she said with excitement.

"What?" I asked incredulously.

"I saw something move under the lawn mower!" Clarissa repeated.

We all watched the bottom of the lawn mower. After a moment, something shifted underneath. It looked to be about the size of a large rat...or a small dog.

My stomach sank. Whatever those things were, they were growing.

The sun was still out, so I wasn't worried about it coming out from underneath the mower. Yet. But, when the sun went down? Yes, I believed it would come out them. Oh, yeah. Of course it would.

That's when the nightmares always come out.

To Phyllis, I said, "Let's go finish loading. Now."

"What is that, Paul? *What is that under there?*"

"I don't know, Phyl, but it was less than three inches long when Ralph threw it up. Let's get moving now, please. I want to get on the road to the cabin before dark."

Keith was already pulling his sister into the house, and I took Phyl's hand. At the garage, I pushed Phyl inside and said, "Go easy on clothes – we can wash them, or wear most for more than one day. Suitcases go into the car's trunk. Load every bit of food we have in the kitchen into the SUV as soon as I turn it around and back it up to the garage. Ice chests are in the kitchen. I'll put down the back seats to give us more room. We'll stop at a supermarket on the way out of town. Now, go...hurry!"

Phyl nodded, and the kids ran to their rooms to pack. As I started to pull away, my wife pulled me back. "Will we be okay, Paul?"

"I certainly hope so, Phyl. But, I won't lie – I just don't know!"

I let go of her hand and went back to the SUV. I kept a wary eye on the lawn mower as I turned the SUV around and backed it to the open garage. As I got out and walked around the vehicle, I happened to glance at the upstairs window next door.

In the Johnsons' upstairs window was a squirmer, but this thing was at least a foot long. It was clinging to the glass, tapping it with its one antenna. One of its six legs was huge, with a pincer-like claw at the end. As I watched, it raised that claw and brought it down on the window with a sharp rap. The glass held, but if that thing got any bigger or stronger, the glass would shatter.

Then it would be loose.

Was this what was lurking under the lawn mower, awaiting its opportunity to escape once the sun was down? And what about the others locked inside

Ralph and Catherine's house? Were they searching for ways out as well? Of course they were! But, unless a window was open, or a vent opened directly to the outside, they couldn't get out. Not until the sun went down. How did they breathe, hatching inside human bodies that way? If they can hold their breaths inside a body, couldn't they...?

I broke into a sprint, dashing into the house. As I slammed open the kitchen door from the garage, I noticed that Phyl was loading an ice chest.

"Where are the kids?" I excitedly asked. "Hurry! Where?"

Puzzled, Phyl said, "In their rooms, I guess. What's wrong?"

"Come on!" I shouted, as I ran down the hall to the stairs.

At the downstairs guest bathroom, I skidded to a halt, and Phyllis stopped behind me. I was watching carefully, and listening with every ounce of hearing that I possessed.

Something was in the toilet. I could hear the water moving quietly.

The lid popped up a couple of inches, then slammed back down.

"Oh, my God," whispered Phyllis, with terror in her voice.

"Go upstairs, and make sure the kids aren't using the bathroom. I got this," I whispered.

The toilet lid popped up another couple of inches, then banged down again.

"*Go!*" I whispered urgently.

Phyllis ran for the stairs.

Now I was faced with the problem of trapping that thing inside the toilet. I thought rapidly, and, as the toilet lid popped up and banged down again, I did the only thing I could think of on short notice.

I flushed.

I heard the creature splashing and floundering as I picture it swirling in a rapid circle as the water went down the hole.

Our guest room still had a thirty-two inch old color television, and it weighed at least fifty pounds. I unplugged it and disconnected the cable from it, took it into the bathroom, and perched the heavy old beast on the toilet lid.

One down. Two to go, and both were upstairs.

"*Paul!* Come up here, quick!" yelled Phyllis from the top of the stairs.

I ran as fast as I could, only stopping to grab a golf club out of the bag of clubs that I'd been meaning to sell and hadn't gotten around to yet. I dashed up the stairs and found Phyllis and Clarissa in the hallway outside the kids' bathroom.

Keith was inside, being bounced up and down as he stood on the toilet seat.

The creature inside this toilet must have been much bigger, because Keith weighed around eighty pounds. He was having trouble keeping his balance with each bounce, and he looked terrified.

"Hold on, buddy!" I shouted.

I ran to our bedroom and opened my closet. On the top shelf, my probing hands found my double-barreled, side-by-side 12-guage shotgun. I pulled it down and broke it open quickly. Then I reached up and found the wooden box that I used to hold ammunition for my shotgun, my rifle, and my .357 Model 19 Smith & Wesson revolver. I grabbed a handful of shotgun shells, loaded two into the gun, and went back to the bathroom.

"Phyllis, when I say the word, you grab Keith and carry him out of the bathroom as fast as you can. I'll shoot the thing if I have to, but maybe we can just close the bathroom door and keep it inside long enough for us to get out of the house."

Phyllis nodded. "Okay, be ready, and be careful, Paul."

I nodded as I shouldered the shotgun. Phyllis went into the bathroom and opened her arms in preparation of grabbing Keith.

I set myself, and said, "Okay, *go!*"

It seemed as if everything moved in slow motion even though it only lasted a few seconds.

Phyllis grabbed our son and dashed for the door of the bathroom. She had made two steps when the lid exploded upward, water splashed out all over, and the creature leapt from the toilet and landed on the floor of the bathroom. Phyllis got out of the bathroom, and the creature turned toward me, as I stood there in the doorway. I had no time to grab the know and close the door, because I could see its back leg muscles bunching for another jump. This thing was the size of a dachshund. Phyllis and Keith had barely cleared the door when I took aim at the creature, and pulled the trigger. The shot caught the creature in mid-jump, and it exploded into black goo that covered the bathroom wall behind it. All six legs detached from its body. The head of the thing landed against the shower curtain, and slowly slid down into the tub, leaving a black, viscous trail as it slid.

The shot had been incredibly loud inside the small room, and my ears were still ringing. I could hear Phyllis and the kids crying. Then I heard Phyllis screaming and pointing toward our bedroom.

Coming out of the bedroom was another one of the squirmers. It had obviously came out of the toilet in the master bathroom.

Phyllis and the kids were scrambling backwards away from the creature. All three were screaming and crying, and the scene threatened to sink into confusion and desperation.

I brought the shotgun to my shoulders again, and pulled the trigger once more. This creature exploded into the same black goo.

I turned toward the bathroom to shut the door, and as I grabbed the knob, I saw small squirmers wiggling around in the goo from the first creature that I had shot. They were all making their way to the bathroom door. I slammed the door, and saw that more of the baby squirmers were coming down the hall from the remains of the second creature.

"Okay, screw this! We're leaving *now!*" I yelled to Phyllis and the kids.

Phyllis grabbed Clarissa's hand, and I took Keith's. We went downstairs. I told them to grab what they could, and to put it in the car. I went to take a peek into the guest bathroom, and the TV was bouncing slightly and rocking back and forth. Something was for sure trying to get out. Right after I slammed the bathroom door shut, I heard the old faithful Sanyo crash to the tiles, and something slammed against the door from the inside.

I didn't wait to see what it was.

I hurried to the kitchen, wishing that I had been able to get my rifle. My .357 revolver was hidden in the cookie jar on top of the refrigerator, so I managed to get it and tuck it under my waistband behind my back. The big ice chest was almost full, so I finished loading it with frozen food, mostly meats, and slammed it shut. I picked it up and carried it to the SUV.

Phyl had the kids safely tucked into the car's back seat. If we made it through the supermarket safely, one of the kids would ride with me.

"Okay, Phyl, we stop at McKelvie's Foods. Keep your cell phone handy, and if it doesn't look safe, we won't go in," I said.

Phyl nodded. "Okay, Paul. Please be careful."

I nodded, and handed her the shotgun after I had loaded it. I also gave her all of the shot shells that I had left...seven. We might have to make another stop on the way to the cabin, just to buy more clothes and some ammunition.

The cabin itself had electricity. It had belonged to my parents. After one of my books had sold really well, I had installed solar cells and batteries, along with three windmills, so the cabin had electricity...at least enough to run a freezer and refrigerator, maybe enough to run a few other things, too.

As I climbed into the driver's seat of the SUV, I couldn't help looking over at the Johnson house one more time. The squirmer was still in the upstairs window, and it seemed bigger. It was still banging that claw against the window, and as I watched, the window cracked.

My beautiful new Cub Cadet lawn mower was rocking back and forth, as if something was anxiously trying to escape.

Yes, it was definitely time to leave.

I started the SUV, pulled down the driveway and into the street. Phyllis followed almost on my bumper. I glanced at the houses across the street. I couldn't help myself.

I didn't see anything at the Millers', but there was a good-sized squirmer in the upstairs front window of the Taylors'. The Taylors lived immediately across the street from the Johnsons, and they also had a corner house. It looked as if the squirmers had traveled the sewers to our place, and the two houses across the street. They may have gone further, but I wasn't turning around to find out. I turned right on Oak, which would take us to the suburbs on the west side of town, where all of the big box stores lived. McKelvie's Foods was there, and the sporting goods store was in the same shopping strip. If they looked clear, Phyl could get food, and I could get ammunition, at least one more shotgun, and a couple of rifles. I thanked God that there was no waiting period for long guns.

My phone rang. It was Phyl.

"Paul, how's the gas in the SUV?" she asked, after I had answered the phone.

I looked at the fuel gauge. "I have a quarter of a tank."

"That's about what I have," Phyllis replied.

"Okay, we'll stop along the way...after we hit McKelvie's."

"Whatever you think, honey. Have you thought to turn on the radio?"

I mentally slapped myself on the forehead. "No, I honestly haven't thought about it."

"Would you mind? I don't want to for a couple of obvious reasons," she said. I knew that she meant the kids.

"Okay, baby, I'll call you back if I learn anything," I said. We disconnected.

I turned on the radio, and pressed the "seek" button. When it stopped on music, I pressed it again. Finally it stopped on an all-news station in our city.

"...backed up all along the east side of the city. If you're heading east, don't take the freeway. If you're heading west into the mountains, everything looks clear right now. We don't know a lot about the bugs, but we have reports coming in from all over. It appears that they first appeared on the outskirts of the east side of the city, and have been working their way steadily west. Emergency officials say that the bugs are growing larger after they're thrown up by infected people. They are carnivorous, and cannibalistic. Leaders are working on a way to kill the bugs, but have been unsuccessful so far. No one knows where they came from, and no one knows whether they're even from this planet. At least, no one official is sharing that information with us. Once again, if you're trying to get out of the city, stay off of the freeway to the east of town. It's one long chain reaction crash, for over a mile or more..."

I snapped the radio off, and called Phyllis. When she answered, I told her what the radio had said, then I said, "Whatever we do, we need to hurry through the supermarket, and I have at least two other places that I want to go. We need ammunition, and we need a laptop, since I didn't have time to grab mine."

I could see Phyl nodding in my rear view mirror, then her voice came. "Okay, Paul. And we can fill both vehicles up a little farther west, if you don't mind."

I chuckled grimly. "I don't mind a bit. I'm hoping that the flow of bugs will slow down once we're out of the city."

"Me, too, honey."

We disconnected.

THE PARKING LOT AT McKelvie's wasn't crowded, and I could see people milling around inside. Michael's Sporting Goods was also open, and I could see a couple of people inside there, too. I parked, and Phyl parked beside me. We all got out of the vehicles, and met beside the shopping cart return.

"Here's what we need to do. Keith, you're coming with me over to Michael's. Clarissa, you go with your mother, and fill up with canned stuff. As much as you can get. Veggies, canned meat, fruit...just whatever. Also, spaghetti sauce, pasta, and Parmesan cheese. Things that will keep without refrigeration. Get butter, because we can freeze it, and a couple of gallons of milk..."

Phyllis held up her hand. "Why don't you and Keith go get the hardware, and meet us inside McKelvie's. That way, you and I can each have a cart, and the kids can have a cart. That should hold most of what we need."

I smiled at my wife. Typical accountant, thinking logically again. "Yes, ma'am. And, Phyl?"

"What, dear?"

I kissed her and said, "Keep your eyes open." I looked down at our daughter. "That goes for you, too, 'rissa."

"Okay, Daddy," said Clarissa.

We parted ways, and Keith and I headed for Michael's.

Chapter 3

Two men were inside Michael's, one was behind the counter, and the other one was just staring out the window.

Keith and I walked to the man behind the counter.

"Afternoon, fellas! What can I do for you?" said the man.

I smiled at him. "Afternoon. We would like a shotgun and two rifles, and we need ammunition, too."

"What kind of shotgun were you looking for? I've got a great deal on a Russian 12-guage single shot this week – only a hundred bucks."

I shook my head. "No, I need a pump, with a magazine that holds about ten shells."

The man smiled. "I have one that I think you'll like." He went to one of the racks on the wall and pulled down a beautiful gun. "Take a look at this one." He handed it to me.

I checked it out, grateful that my family had always used guns, both for hunting and for sports. I loved them, and I enjoyed target shooting. Keith had been shooting for just over a year now, and I had just given Clarissa her second lesson. Both were taking to it like ducks take to water.

I showed Keith how and where to load the gun, and what to do to pump a shell into the chamber.

I handed it back to the man, and told him we'd take it.

"Great! That's the shotgun! Now, what kind of rifles were you interested in?"

"I want a thirty-ought six, and is that an SKS with a wooden stock that I see over there?" I pointed to the rifle that I was talking about.

"Good eye! Yep, that's a Russian. Shoots 7.62 x 54 cartridges. It came with a thirty-round magazine, and I think I have another that will fit it in the back room. The only brand of thirty-ought six that I have is Remington, with ten-round clips."

"Sold." I picked up a pad and wrote on it. "Here's the list of ammo I need, and I'll take all you can sell me."

The man whistled. "Mister, you just made my week! My name's Michael Hayes. I own this place." He held out his hand.

I shook hands, and said, "I'm Paul Stiles. This is my son, Keith."

Michael tilted his head. "Paul Stiles, the writer?"

I nodded.

"Well, I will be damned! I'm reading your latest book right now!" He pointed to a tablet he had put down on the counter when we came in.

I smiled. "Thank you so much. I hope you're enjoying it."

"Oh, yeah! I love me some Stiles stuff!" He dug out some forms and handed them to me. "Well, here's the paperwork. And I need to see your driver's license so that I can call in the background check."

I handed him my driver's license, and I filled out the paperwork while Michael called in my information.

Fifteen minutes later, we were ready to pay for our hardware. I was leaning against the counter when I happened to see something half hidden on the shelf.

It was a flare gun, still in the original box.

Michael totaled my purchases, and was about to tell me the amount when I said, "I'll take that flare gun, too...and all of the flares that you have in stock."

"Mr. Stiles, you just paid my rent for the month," replied Michael, as he added everything up.

I put it all on my credit card. I handed Keith the two rifles and I tucked the shotgun under my arm. I had bought another wooden ammo box, and it was full to the brim. Michael picked up the rest of our purchases, and said, "I'll help you carry this stuff out."

We got up front, and the other man was still standing in the same spot.

I asked Michael if the man was okay, and Michael said, "Sure. He came in earlier, and said that he didn't feel well, and asked if he could just stay for a few minutes until he felt better. I told him that would be fine."

I nodded, and the three of us carried the hardware out of the store and loaded it into the SUV.

As we loaded, I asked Michael, whose last name was Thomas, what he was going to do about the bugs.

He didn't know what I was talking about. He hadn't heard anything, and hadn't had the radio or television on that day. He usually surfed the internet at night, after the shop was closed and he had gone home.

I told him about my day, and what I had heard on the radio. Then, I told him where we were going. He was incredulous.

Keith was the convincer. He said, "Mr. Thomas, one of those things almost got me and my mom. It came up through the toilet, and Dad shot it with the shotgun. They're big, and ugly, and scary. It's okay if you don't want to believe it, but don't not believe it too long, because they'll get you if you're not careful."

We had walked back to the front of the sporting goods store. We all three happened to look up at the same time, and we saw the man that had stayed in the store.

He bent over at the waist and vomited an ungodly amount of blood and black ichor.

"Oh, dear God," I said. "Keith, let's go get the ladies."

Michael, the sporting goods man, was staring in at the mess the man had made in the front window. Squirmers were wiggling around in the goo that had splattered on the window and on the display, and the man had collapsed onto the floor below our line of sight. Michael looked stunned.

"That's how it started for me today," I said. I made a fast decision. "Michael, you have a while before those things become able to move around outside of the goo. If you want to come with us, we'll go get what we can *while* we can out of your shop. The invitation's there, man. You just have to make up your mind fast."

"My van is parked right over there. I'll pull it around to the shop, if you'll help me load the artillery," said Michael.

"You're on," I told him. To Keith, I said, "Go find your mom and tell her what happened here. Tell her that we're bringing Michael with us, and we'll be over to the store as soon as we can get artillery loaded."

"Okay, Dad," Keith replied, eyes wide with the sight of all the goo. Oh, well, it was inevitable that he would see it happen, as fast as things were moving. Off he went to find his mother inside McKelvie's.

Michael got his van pulled around in front of the sporting goods store. When he joined me at the store's front door, I said, "Don't step in any of the blood or black goo. I saw a cop do that today, and one of those squirmy things crawled to him, went up his pants, and burrowed into his leg. I can't stress to you enough how dangerous those things are, and how dangerous they become."

"Okay, let's do this. What do we need besides artillery? I have lots of MREs and other survivalist stuff."

"Let's get those for sure, and we'll take whatever else we think we can use."

We shared a look, and went inside.

That familiar smell hit me once again, and Michael gagged from either the smell or the goo – I wasn't sure which. Either one was enough to cause it. The blood and goo had splattered, but the splatter was in the window and on the glass. Very little was on the floor, and for that, I was grateful.

You have never seen two men load a van as quickly as we did. We grabbed ice chests, canteens, and even sleeping bags. There were lots of cases of MREs, and we gathered all of those that Michael had in stock. We loaded guns, ammunition, and hearing protection. We loaded goggles and hunting knives, bows and arrows. And we somehow got it all inside that van.

When we left the store, the squirmers had just begun dropping off of the dais that served as the window display area, and began moving across the floor. Michael closed the door and locked it firmly.

"Now what, Paul?" he asked.

"Let's move your van over beside the SUV and the car, then we'll head inside McKelvie's. How's that?"

Michael nodded. "Sounds good."

We got the van parked, and headed inside the supermarket.

It was not crowded at all. The store had few customers, fewer than on a normal night. We passed one of the bagboys, and I said to him, "Sure is quiet tonight."

The boy nodded. "Yes, sir, it is. I don't know what's going on, but we haven't had many customers all afternoon long."

"Wow," I said, or something like that.

Michael and I each pulled out a shopping cart, and began searching for Phyllis and the kids. As we passed the juice aisle, Michael said, "Do you think we should load up on this, too?"

I nodded. "Can't hurt, can it? We don't know how long we'll be at the cabin, so load it up!"

Michael began filling his buggy, and I continued on to find Phyllis. She and the kids were two aisles over, in front of the canned soup.

"Daddy!" yelled Clarissa excitedly.

"Hi, Dad!" said Keith. "Did you guys get everything that we needed?"

"We sure did, son! Michael has a van, and it's filled to the brim! Hi, honey," I said to Phyllis. I put an arm around her shoulders and kissed her.

"So, I hear you've made a friend," she said.

I nodded. "He's coming with us, Phyl. We can sure use the help."

"And the supplies." In a low voice, she said, "Was it bad?"

"Yes. The bugs had just started moving out of the goo when we knocked off."

She shook her head, as if to say, "Unbelievable."

"Yeah, we need to hurry. I don't want to be here when they get bigger," I said.

Phyl had two carts. She had one that was partially full, and the cart that the kids were pushing was overloaded with cans of food, bottles of water, and boxes of things like crackers and pasta that would stay edible for a long time.

She had also gotten both powdered milk and evaporated milk. I hadn't even thought of getting those.

"Paul, should we go now?" Phyllis asked, concern showing on her face.

"No, we have time. But let's hurry."

We filled up her buggy and mine, and met up with Michael, who had filled his buggy with juice, and other non-perishable goods.

When we got to the checkouts, only two were open. One was staffed by a teenage girl, and the other was staffed by a middle-aged woman. Neither one was busy, so we took the teenager, and Michael took the middle-aged woman. The two teen bagboys started bagging our purchases.

"Wow! You guys sure are buying a lot of groceries!" said our checkout girl. Her nametag read "Teresa". "I don't think I've ever done this much stuff for one customer before!" She totaled the purchase, and, as I was paying with my plastic, Clarissa nudged me.

"Daddy," she whispered.

"What is it, sweetheart?"

"Look," whispered Clarissa again, and she pointed toward the back.

On the light hood over the meat counter was a bug. But this was a new kind of bug that I hadn't seen before.

It had wings. Long, powerful looking, see-through membranes, with veins running throughout. It had a long, sharp-looking proboscis, and one long antenna coming from the center of its head. Its eyes were, as nearly as I could tell at that distance, were solid black. Its attention was focused on the meat inside the counter. As I watched, it jumped down into the meats and began sticking that proboscis into the packages. It was about the size of a Jack Russell terrier.

"Oh, *shit*," I whispered.

Phyllis heard me, and so did Teresa.

"What is it, Paul?" asked Phyllis.

I put my finger to my lips in the universal "shushing" gesture, then I pointed to the back.

Phyllis looked for a moment, not seeing it. It moved, and caught her attention. The color drained from her face.

"Paul," she said quietly, "we have to get these people out of here...take them with us."

I tallied up the space we'd have, and nodded. We had room.

Teresa leaned over to see what we were watching. When she saw it, she drew in a sharp intake of air, about to scream. I clamped my hand over her mouth and started whispering.

"Teresa, don't scream. I don't know what attracts those things, but we can't take a chance that sound will bring it up to us. Do you understand?"

Teresa nodded. While I was talking to her, Phyllis got the bagboy's attention, and showed him. Michael saw it, too, and showed it to the middle-aged lady – "Millie" was what her name tag read. The kids showed the last bagboy.

"Now, listen carefully," I said. "The whole city is being gradually overcome by bugs – it's on the news and the radio. They're working their way west. We have a cabin in the mountains. That's where we're going, and Michael is coming, too. We want you to come with us, very quietly, because that thing will soon be joined by more. We have to go now. Drop everything, and let's go."

Teresa, Millie, and our bagboy, Richie, nodded their heads, and began to help us push the carts. The other bagboy, Tommy, wasn't fazed.

"I ain't afraid of no bug," he said defiantly, with all the bluster a seventeen-year-old kid could muster. "I'm gonna kill that fuckin' thing."

I stopped, and motioned the others to go ahead. Out the door they went. I turned to Tommy.

"Tommy, I have no idea what that thing can do, but I strongly think you should reconsider, son," I said quietly. "No harm, no foul, okay? Come on, let's go."

"Fuck that! And fuck you, mister!" Tommy had picked up a mop from a display in front of the windows. He broke the mop head off of the stick, and whacked the floor with it. "No damn bug is going to scare me!"

I caught a glimpse of something moving through the air extremely fast, and the bug flew past Tommy and smacked into the window. It righted itself, and buzzed Tommy again. He waved the mop handle at the thing and missed.

Then I heard a sound that sent chills down my spine. It sounded like a beehive, but it was as if the sound was playing through an amplifier. It was loud enough to vibrate the floor, and it was coming from the direction of the meat counter.

"Tommy!" I shouted from right beside the door. "We have to go *now!*" And I ducked out the door, which automatically closed behind me.

I heard Tommy shout, "No way!"

I looked back as I ran, and I saw three of the flying bugs zipping around Tommy. I stopped, fascinated by what I was seeing. They were circling around him, buzzing close to his head each time. Tommy swung the mop handle several times, but kept missing the bugs. Finally, one of them flew close enough to hit Tommy's head. It must have bit him when it hit him, because blood started to flow from Tommy's head in a gush. He seemed dazed by the hit, and he continued to swing the mop handle in futility. Another bug, or maybe the same one, hit him again, and knocked him to the floor. The bug dropped out of sight, followed by the other two. I didn't go back to look.

I hurried the last few steps to the vehicles, shaking my head as I went.

Teresa timidly asked, "Is Tommy coming?"

"No, Tommy won't be coming," I replied.

Teresa began to cry quietly.

We got everything packed into the three vehicles. I don't think we could have gotten anything else inside them when we were done. As it was, people were going to have to scrunch together in the car. As we were climbing into the vehicles, the sun was just beginning to touch the horizon.

We all heard a loud thump. It had come from McKelvie's, and it was the sound of something hitting one of the huge glass windows. We all turned to look, and what we saw there chilled us to the bone.

There wasn't an empty spot on the window inside the store. Flying bugs were covering it, fluttering their wings, and shifting their positions. We could hear tapping, and I noticed that a couple of the bugs were tapping the window sharply with their proboscises. If they all started tapping, the window could break. Or, they could find the automatic door, which would be worse.

"Okay, time to go," I said. I gave instructions. "We won't go by the freeway, because it will only be a matter of time before it's completely blocked. We'll take highway 72 all the way to Pine Valley, in the mountains. We'll go to the cabin from there." I started to get into the SUV, then turned back. "We have to stop for gas. There's a town, Murray, twenty miles down the highway. We'll stop there."

A quick glance at Michael's Sporting Goods told us even more. The window there was covered with squirmers that were the size of rats.

I led the way out of the parking lot. Keith and Richie rode with me in the front seat. Phyllis was second in line, driving the car. She had Clarissa and Teresa with her. Michael brought up the rear, driving the van, with Millie in the passenger seat. We didn't bring anyone else's car because we were going to have enough trouble finding gasoline for three vehicles. That, and we didn't want to get too spread out from each other. We had all exchanged cell phone numbers, and Michael had brought some portable radios that he had in stock. We each had one of those, and brand new batteries to keep them powered. Their range wasn't great, but they were better than nothing in case the cell phones stopped working.

We turned on the radio. The all-news station wasn't on the air, but other stations were. The story had become big enough for the Emergency Alert System to be activated.

"...and all residents are urged to stay indoors. The President has ordered the National Guard activated in all fifty states to try to stop the bug advance.

There seem to be several different species, and they aren't true insects. These creatures have lungs, and are warm-blooded. Scientists suspect that the bugs have hitchhiked their way to earth on a meteor, although they bear strong resemblances to insects from the Jurassic and other prehistoric periods. DNA is being coded by top government scientists in an effort to discover..." I clicked the radio off.

I noticed that Richie had his cell phone out.

"Richie, you want to try to call your parents or something? Let them know that you're all right?" I asked.

Richie stared out the window for a moment before he answered me. "I did. Both phones went straight to voicemail." He turned to me with tears in his eyes. "We live in one of the subdivisions. Maple Meadows."

That was four blocks over from our house.

"Maybe they were at work, Richie," I said.

"They both work evenings, Mr. Stiles. They don't go in until seven."

I watched the road for a couple of beats. "I'm sorry, son."

"Thank you, sir. And thank you for saving us."

We rode in silence for a few minutes.

Keith said, "Dad, is this the end of the world?"

I smiled and said, "No, Keith."

"But what if the bugs kill everyone?"

"The world will go on. Besides, we aren't dead yet. And we won't be, if I have anything to say about it."

Chapter 4

We stopped in Murray to gas up. The little convenience store looked lit up and open, and the gas pumps were working, but no one was inside...at least, no one that we could see.

There were enough pumps so that we all parked under the brightly lit canopy. Phyllis pumped her gas, Michael pumped his, and Richie pumped ours. I stood off to the side, keeping watch. I was terrified that we'd be caught out in the open.

"Everybody fill the tanks to the brim!" I said. "We don't want to have to stop again until we get to the cabin!"

I felt that I was preaching to the choir. Everyone already knew to fill up. It was only my nervousness that made me repeat it.

I can't tell you how nervous those flying bugs made me feel. Ever since we saw them, all I could think of was the phrase "death from above". Crawling bugs were one thing, but flying bugs represented a completely different set of circumstances. The sun had set, but it was still dusk. It was bright enough that I could see the skies, and I didn't see any flying bugs.

My mind kept whirling around what the radio had said about the bugs having lungs, and that they were warm-blooded. Scientists had said for years that the only reason that insects didn't grow bigger was because they didn't have lungs. Were these bugs something that had been genetically altered in some laboratory, and had escaped? Or were they mutations that had stayed in hiding until their numbers grew? Or, no matter how outlandish, had they really hitched a ride on a meteor and come from somewhere in space?

It seemed as if no one really knew for sure. Given time, government scientists could code the DNA from these things, and maybe have a better idea about them. But what could we do in the meantime?

I shook my head, symbolically trying to get rid of those thoughts. I needed to focus on the here and now, and help keep eight people alive. In our situation, it's not day-to-day, or even hour-to-hour. It's minute-by-minute.

"We're all filled up, Paul!" called Phyllis. "Do we need to go inside for anything?"

We had all paid with plastic at the pump, so I said, "Not unless we need something."

Michael spoke up. "I could sure use a cup of coffee."

"Me, too," added Millie.

As it turned out, everyone needed something to drink.

"Okay, someone has to stay out here and keep watch. I think it should be either Michael or me," I said.

"All I need is one large black coffee," said Michael. "If you'll bring it out to me, I'll keep watch."

We agreed, so we all went inside the store.

No one was inside. It was deserted, but there was a television on over the counter, and on it were pictures and videos of the advancing bugs. We all stopped and watched. There was no sound, but none was needed. There were creatures that looked like millipedes, with huge, pincer-like jaws. Some of the bugs looked like a cross between a mosquito and a duck, with both a long, sharp proboscis, a bill, and feathery wings. There were videos of the city being overrun, and many of the videos were security camera footage. No news footage was shown, probably because of the danger.

The picture shifted to a news anchor, and Richie found the remote for the television, and turned up the sound.

"...and the Islamic Holy Army in Iraq has stated that they are responsible for the release of these hybrid monsters on what they called, 'the Western infidels'. It has been suggested that Russian scientists, under the control of the Russian Mafia, developed the creatures for money. The Iraqi government denies any involvement, and denounces this action..."

"That's enough," I said. "Turn it off, please, Richie."

He did.

"Well, that explains where they came from," said Phyllis. "They're genetic mutations, created by some dumbass Russians. But how did they multiply so much, and so quickly?"

"I don't know, and I don't care," I replied. "Let's just get our stuff and get out of here."

No one argued with that. We all chose our drinks, and Millie got the coffee for Michael. At the front, Millie asked, "Should we pay for this stuff?"

I had a twenty in my wallet. I pulled it out and put it on the cash register.

"That will cover our drinks," I said. "If no one collects it, it isn't our fault, and we've done nothing wrong." I pointed to the security camera. "There's our proof that we paid, if it ever comes up."

As we left the convenience store, Michael stopped us. "Listen."

We listened. We heard nothing. And I said as much to Michael.

"You're right. Nothing. No traffic, no dogs barking, no people noises of any kind," said Michael. "Doesn't that strike you as odd?"

I began to get nervous. "Yes, it does. Let's get going."

As we passed through Murray, we didn't see a single car or person. Or dog, for that matter.

THINGS WERE DIFFERENT when we got to Pine Valley. Our little caravan was only one of many. It seemed as if everyone from miles around were passing through the town on their way to hopeful safety, away from the advancing bugs. Traffic was horrendous, but we managed to stay together.

I used the radio to call to Phyllis and Michael, and I said, "The turnoff is a mile and a half ahead. Turn right on Route Sixteen. It goes up into the mountains. We'll make two more turns after that. Let's stay as close together as we can."

Both Phyllis and Michael responded in the affirmative.

We drove at a snail's pace, and we never did find out what was up ahead causing the traffic to travel so slow, because we got to Route Sixteen before we found the reason. We turned right on Sixteen, and began our upward climb. The Rocky Mountains are absolutely beautiful, but the night was dark, and we could only see what our headlights highlighted. We met no traffic coming down the mountain.

We got to the first turn, and we turned right onto County Road Number Eight. We traveled two point seven miles, then turned left onto the dirt-and-gravel road that let to our cabin. There were no electric lines here, no telephone poles marching off to nowhere and everywhere to litter the landscape. There were only the mountains, the trees, and the underbrush. We hoped that there were no bugs.

As we rounded the last curve on the gravel road, the cabin came into sight. It was a beautiful sight, a two-story A-frame cabin with wooden shingles and wooden siding, all hand-hewn from trees that came from the forest around it. It had been built by my great-grandfather back in the thirties, before anyone else lived on the mountain. We had neighbors now, however. A couple of women shared another cabin just a bit further along the road. They lived there year-round, and we had always been friendly with them. They looked after the place for us when we weren't there, so, of course they had keys.

There were three outbuildings. One outbuilding housed the well, and another contained the batteries and gasoline generator that we used when the wind was still, and the sky was overcast. It didn't get used often, but it had an automatic switch that fired it up if the batteries got below a certain amount. The third outbuilding contained a sizeable walk-in freezer. The twin windmills, one on the north side of the cabin, and one on the south side, were spinning in the breeze that was coming down from the top of the mountain. There were several banks of solar cells tilted slightly toward the south. Between the windmills and the solar cells, we rarely had to use the generator.

The freezer came to be before the kids were born. Phyllis and I decided to spend a four day weekend at the cabin years ago, during the last week of September. She had taken off a Friday and the following Monday. We brought just enough food to last the weekend. On Sunday night, an early snow that surprised everyone trapped us on the mountain for the next week. We were able to stretch our food to last until we could leave the cabin, but the next summer, we bought the walk-in freezer, had it delivered to the cabin, and we built a secure outbuilding around a concrete floor to keep it in. We also stocked it completely, and renewed the stock every year. It was the only thing at the cabin that was kept running year round. That, and the refrigerator inside the cabin.

We parked the vehicles side-by-side, as close to the porch steps on that side as possible. We all climbed out, and stood stretching our tense muscles. And listening to the night's sounds.

The normal sound of the breeze coming down the mountain and the turning blades chopping the wind were the two main sounds. No insects could be heard, and no animal sounds from the forest came to our ears. That could be either good or bad.

The lack of insect noise bothered me, though. I felt that the lack of it gave me goosebumps.

When we finished stretching, moaning, and loosening our sore bodies, Michael said, "What do we unload first?"

"Nothing. Yet," I said.

"Something wrong, Paul?" asked Michael.

I shrugged. "We just need to check everything out first. Come on, you and me. We'll take the outbuildings first."

"You're the man."

We each took a shotgun. Richie asked for one, too. I gave it to him. He started to come with us, and I stopped him, and pulled him over to the side.

"Richie, I need you to stay here, please."

"Why, Mr. Stiles?" he asked. "I can handle one of these as good as either of you."

"I have no doubts about that, son." I pointed. "Look there. Three women, and two kids. Phyllis can handle a gun just as well as I can, but she needs help. I've got Michael. Phyllis has you. I need you to stay with them, and help protect the group. Understand?"

He followed my line of reasoning, and came to the same conclusion. "You're right, sir. I have to say, you're pretty smart for a writer!"

"That's why they call us special snowflakes, Richie," I replied.

We rejoined Michael, and I said, "Michael, Richie is staying here with the group. He's going to help Phyllis keep everyone safe."

Michael, bless his heart, caught on quickly. "Good. One less thing for you and I to worry about, with Richie here." He looked at Richie. "Don't aim that at anything you don't intend to shoot if you have to, and don't shoot anything you don't intend to kill. Or anybody. You gonna be okay, kid?"

Richie nodded, holding the shotgun across the front of his body, with the barrel pointed up. "Yes, sir!"

I went over to Phyllis. "We're going to check out the outbuildings, and then the cabin. Richie's going to stay here with you."

Phyllis looked into my eyes. "You be careful, Paul Stiles."

"You be careful, too, Phyllis Stiles."

I kissed her quickly on the lips, and headed over to the battery building. I had the keys to the padlock, so I opened the lock, and on a count of "one, two, three", I swung the door open. Nothing in there that shouldn't have been.

We moved to the well house, and repeated the process. Nothing.

We moved to the solid little building that had been built around the walk-in freezer. We checked inside. Nothing.

It was time to check the cabin. For some reason that I couldn't fathom, I was nervous. Goosebumps had sprung out all over. Just then, my cellphone rang.

During the warm months, we had cell service at the cabin. One of the companies had leased some land on the mountain, and built a tower there. They had also installed generators and solar cells to keep the equipment working. Once the snow fell, all bets were off.

So, we had phone service. I still jumped when it rang, because it startled me.

I looked at the number, but I didn't recognize it. I answered.

"Hello?" I said.

"Stiles? Paul Stiles?" said the voice on the other end.

"That's me," I replied.

"This is Bobby Barnes. Is that offer still good about your cabin?"

It was the cop that I had met earlier. He must have made it out of the city, too.

"You bet it is, Bobby! Where are you?"

"We just turned right onto Sixteen."

"We?" I asked.

Bobby laughed. "Yeah, I picked up a few stragglers on the way. You won't believe what one of them is bringing! Might be a big help to us later!"

"You're just a few minutes away, Bobby. Come on up the mountain, and we'll see what's what. How's that?"

"Sounds good. We'll be right there!"

"Hey, Bobby, look for my wife, Phyllis. I've picked up some folks, too, and two of us are going inside to check the cabin. You know, make sure that it's safe."

"We'll be right there, Paul! Just watch for us!"

I disconnected, and said to Michael, "I have to talk to Phyl. Come with me. You need to hear this."

I pulled the group around and said, "That call was the cop that helped me earlier. I had invited him here this morning, and gave him directions. He's just turned onto Sixteen, and should be here in a few minutes. He said that he's picked up a few people along the way, and I told him that was fine." I looked at Phyl. "I told him to look for you, because Michael and I would be checking out the cabin."

"Where do you want them to park?" she asked.

"Close to the cabin. As close as possible."

Phyl nodded, and I turned to Michael.

"Ready?"

"Ready as I'll ever be," said Michael.

"Let's go, then."

We walked to the porch steps. We climbed them, and stopped on the welcome mat outside the front door. I tried the knob before I started unlocking the lock. It's a habit I have that I can't seem to get rid of. I know, because I've tried.

The front door was unlocked.

Now, normally, that wouldn't mean much, and it wouldn't bother me. Maybe it only meant that Susan and Cheryl, our neighbors just up the mountain, had come down to check on the cabin and forgot to lock the door when they left. For some reason, it disturbed me this time. It disturbed me a great deal.

I shared a look with Michael, and quietly said, "Be ready for anything, buddy."

He nodded.

We went in. We both held shotguns, because they do the most damage at short range. Michael took the left, I took the right, and we scanned the living room. Nothing was out of place. I nodded to Michael, and we began stealthily working our way through the main floor. It was a large cabin, with large, open living room, dining room, and kitchen. A short hallway led to a den that Phyl and I both used as an office, the downstairs bathroom, and the master bedroom. Since most of the living room, dining room, and kitchen were all so open, we could see in the dim light that all of it was clear. Everything looked untouched.

We made our way to the short hallway. The first door we came to was a closet. Nothing was hiding inside, except clothing and junk that we had stored here over the years. The next door was the bathroom. We swung the door open, and both of us froze for a moment.

In the bathtub was Cheryl, one of our two lady neighbors. She was totally out of her head, and her eyes were milky. Empty.

Michael and I both swung our shotguns up and aimed in her general direction. Her mouth was moving, but nothing was coming out. After seeing the same thing with Ralph earlier, I knew what that meant.

I flipped on the light. Cheryl hadn't vomited yet. But it was close.

"Michael, we've got to get her out of the house *now*," I whispered with some urgency. "She's close to spewing squirmers!"

"Doesn't look like she's going to walk if you tell her to," said Michael.

I cocked my head and thought about it. "You know, she just might, if we lead her out." I paused. "If we hurry."

"I have no plans to touch her."

"Neither do I."

"What do we do?"

"We each take one of her hands, and we lead her out of the cabin."

"I'm not touching her, Paul!"

"Hang on, hang on...I got it! Be right back!"

I left the bathroom and went to the closet. I dug around, and, sure enough, my memory had been correct. Two big pairs of thick snow gloves were inside the closet. I grabbed them, and brought them back to the bathroom. I gave a pair to Michael.

"Now," I said to Michael. "We'll each take her by the hand, and we'll lead her outside."

We approached Cheryl, each of us with a hand out.

"Hi, Cheryl," I said gently.

Her head turned toward me as I spoke her name, and those empty eyes looked in my direction from inside her doomed body.

"It's Paul. This nice man with me is Michael. We'd like you to come outside with us. Can you take our hands? We'll help you."

She raised her hands, but we could see that it took her a great deal of effort. Michael and I each took one of Cheryl's hands, and we literally pulled her to her feet.

"Okay, Cheryl, can you lift your left leg over the side of the tub?" I said.

Cheryl raised her leg high – almost high enough to touch her chest with her knee. She stretched it out over the side of the tub, and put it down on the bathroom floor.

"Great, sweetie, now the other leg," I said gently.

She got the other leg out of the bathtub. Michael and I started walking her to the door.

I could hear several vehicle engines outside, coming up the road and parking in the grass. One engine sounded like the diesel on a big truck, and it was struggling to make it up the mountain's grade.

Slowly, ever so slowly, Michael and I walked Cheryl through the living room, and I gave her words of encouragement as we went. Words like, "Good girl" or "almost there, don't stop now" were mantras that I chanted to my former neighbor, hoping and praying that we got her out of the cabin before she threw up her load of squirmers.

A figure appeared in the front door. It was Bobby, still wearing his police uniform. He had his sidearm drawn, and he held it in both hands with the barrel pointed upward.

"Hey, Bobby," I said quietly.

Bobby's eyes snapped to us, and saw that we were leading Cheryl.

"Bobby, remember Ralph? My neighbor? Well, this is Cheryl. She lives just above us here on the mountain," I said. "She seems to have something in common with Ralph, and I'd say we only have a couple of minutes."

Bobby's eyes widened, and then he nodded. "Understood, Paul. I'll make sure that everyone is out of the way. Any particular place you want to take her?"

"Just outside."

Bobby said, "I have something that might help, if you aren't squeamish. I'll go get it."

"Right now, we'll take all the help we can get, Sergeant Barnes," I said, not without some irony.

"I'll be waiting," he said, with a grim look on his face. Then he was gone.

"Nice enough guy," said Michael. "He's been in the shop a couple of times, checking out the handguns."

"He told me almost everything he knew this morning about the bugs," I said. "He was the first cop on the scene when Ralph thr...uh, came over." I said this last part just in case Cheryl was still cognizant enough to comprehend what I was saying. I knew she understood simple terms, but I wasn't going to take a chance of letting her know that her time was almost up.

We got her to the front door and out onto the porch. As we got her to the bottom of the steps, I looked around for Bobby. He was standing off to the side, about fifteen feet away from the cabin. He had what looked like a large pack strapped to his back, with a long hose attached.

"Bring her here, Paul," said Bobby.

"What's that thing on your back, Bobby?" I asked.

"It's a flamethrower."

My eyes widened as I realized what he was going to do.

"Bobby, she's still alive! You can't be serious!" I yelled.

"Paul, you know as well as I do that she's already dead! You saw your neighbor this morning! Once he puked out his guts, he curled up and died!"

"That doesn't mean you can burn her alive!"

"I can, and I will!" Bobby yelled back.

Michael had already let go of Cheryl's hand and backed away.

I was about to yell at Bobby again, when Cheryl opened her mouth and said, "Glrk-k-k..."

I knew what that meant. I dropped her hand, jumped away, and screamed, "Bobby! Go!"

As Cheryl bent at the waist, Bobby's flames hit her. Everything that came out of her mouth boiled away before it hit the ground. Cheryl was still bent over, but flames covered her body, burning it quickly inside a roaring inferno.

She never made a sound.

Bobby hit her again with the flames, and burned a circle of ground around her, too. He wasn't taking chances, and I can't say that I really blamed him. My head had known that he had been right. It had been my heart that had found it hard to go through with what had to be done.

For a few minutes, the only sound that could be heard was the crackling of flames, and the quiet sobbing of my wife.

I looked at Bobby and Michael. "Ready?"

Both looked puzzled.

Michael said, "Ready for what?"

"We have to make certain the rest of the cabin is clear. Then, we need to find Susan. She was our other neighbor."

THE REST OF THE CABIN was clear. No creatures, and no Susan.

Bobby had brought people with him. One guy was driving a cement truck. An eighteen-wheeler had a load of lumber, and its driver was a lady. Another guy drove a big, eighteen-wheel tanker.

The tanker was full of gasoline.

Also, Bobby had brought an RV with ten people, and a delivery van with six more. The delivery van was a milk truck. I saw dairy in everyone's future for a few days, since the milk would go bad quickly.

Bobby had told us that things in the city got really bad before he got out. The creatures were everywhere, and it seemed that no one was secure.

Bugs can get into almost anything, you see.

Bobby had gotten three flamethrowers from the National Guard Armory on the outskirts of the city. The Guard had been called out, but the call came too late for any Guard members to make it to the facility. Bobby had helped himself, with the help of some of the people that came with him. He had driven his patrol car, and they had loaded it with National Guard grenades, missile launchers, machine guns, and lots of ammunition.

Bobby's young partner hadn't made it.

They were called to another bug location, but this one had been growing for a while. It had been one of the millipede-looking creatures, with the long, pincer jaws. It had caught the young cop with both jaws, and, when the jaws spread, they ripped him apart. The creature then ate the pieces.

It was that event that told Bobby it was time to bail. Dying in the line of duty was fine, and he was prepared to do it...*if* it would make a difference.

Against these invading creatures, his death would only have been a small meal for some large bug.

The guy driving the cement truck was Bobby's brother, Billy. The rest of the people had come from a diner just outside of the city. Bobby had told them what was going on, and invited them along. He had come up with an idea for the wood, the cement, and the gasoline, and said that he would explain it later.

We were about to go to Susan's cabin, to find out what had happened to her, and if Cheryl had been there. Our silent prayer was that Susan was okay.

I gathered the group together and, at the risk of seeming to be an asshole, reminded everyone that the cabin belonged to Phyllis and me. Anything major had to be cleared through one of us, and ours was the final say. I don't think I needed to remind any of them of the other option available, should they choose to ignore that basic rule. I left Phyllis in charge, and me, Michael, Bobby, and Richie would go investigate the other cabin.

We made sure that the ones remaining had weapons, and were all loaded and ready. I told Phyllis to get them all started unloading trucks, and figuring out where everyone would sleep.

The four of us began our hike up the mountain.

Chapter 5

It wasn't a long trek. It was less than a quarter-mile. But, it was all uphill. Steep, dark, and rocky uphill.

When we got to the snug little cabin shared by Cheryl and Susan, we saw a light burning in the upstairs window. I held up my hand, indicating that we all should stop...none of us had the breath to say it. We stood in the front yard of the cabin, heaving air into our lungs.

All of us except Richie. Show-off.

My breathing finally returned to a semblance of normal. I said, "Wait a minute. Let me try something." The other three nodded. I shouted, "Susan! Susan, are you in there?"

The curtains fluttered in the upstairs window, and then Susan's face appeared. She raised the window and called, "Paul? Is that you?"

"It's me, Susan. Can you come down?"

"Give me a minute, and I'll be right there," she said, and closed the window.

The cabin that Susan and Cheryl shared was just a bit larger than ours. It had one more outbuilding that we did, several more solar cells than we had, and an extra windmill. These ladies liked their electric comforts.

They had spoken of getting married soon, since the laws against it had been mostly repealed. I was not looking forward to telling her about Cheryl.

The porch light suddenly snapped on, and the front door opened. Susan came out onto the porch dressed in jeans, boots, and a flannel shirt. Her long yellow hair was tied into a ponytail. She was almost forty, but looked to be in her late twenties. She was a gorgeous woman.

Susan was also a worried woman.

"Oh, Paul, I didn't know you were coming, can you help me? Cheryl went to the city on a shopping trip early this morning. I went for a hike this afternoon, and I got back around dusk. Cheryl's Jeep was parked in the garage, but she's nowhere to be found! And this bug thing was all over the news on the satellite channels, and I'm worried sick about her! You haven't seen her, have you?"

Here it was. Do you have any idea how hard it is to break someone's heart the way I was about to break Susan's? And I couldn't ask any of the others to do it. She was my friend, and my neighbor, and it had to be me.

I took each of her hands in each of mine, and I looked her directly in the eye. "Yes, Susan. I've seen her."

A huge look of relief appeared on her face. "Oh, thank God!" she said. "Where did you see her, Paul?"

I hesitated. "She was down at my place, Susan. I found her in my bathtub."

She looked puzzled. "Your bathtub? What was she doing at your place? What's wrong with *our* bathtub?"

I looked over at Michael, then Richie, then Bobby. They all looked away as I looked at them. "Susan, what...uh, how much...what do you know about these bugs?"

With a confused look, she said, "I know that they've wiped out most of the eastern two-thirds of the country. They're all over Europe, Canada, South America, and parts of Russia and China. They've been spotted in Israel and Egypt, too. They're genetically mutated, and they were released by some Islamic crazy group."

I was shocked. I didn't realize that the release had been worldwide. That was scary.

"What else, Susan?"

"They're stopped at the base of the Rockies, and other mountainous areas. It seems to be too cold for them."

"What do you know about people infections?"

"Well, no one knows how the infections first started, but they say that when a person is infected, they lose control of their speech centers, their eyes turn a milky white, and seem empty, like there's no one inside. They said that the reason for that is that the eggs have hatched, and are feeding on portions of the brain, heart, and other organs. Just before they die, they vomit up blood, bugs, and more eggs, and then they..." She stopped abruptly. She had been watching my face, and must have seen something there...like the truth about Cheryl. "Oh,

God," she said in a very small voice. "Paul, no. Not Cheryl. Please, God, no, not her. Not sweet Cheryl."

I held her hands tightly, and nodded.

Susan grabbed me, buried her face in my shoulder, and began crying hard. She was crying as if she had lost her soul. Or, perhaps, just her soulmate. Her sobs were loud and were wrung from the deepest part of her. I held her as tightly as I could, and rubbed her hair to calm her, comfort her, and help her through her grief.

Michael, Richie, and Bobby stood quietly, looking everywhere and nowhere, obviously feeling embarrassed to be witness to this poor woman's terrible grief, and feeling helpless, not knowing how to offer comfort to her.

After I let Susan cry for a few moments, I couldn't shake the feeling that we needed to get back. That we should begin fortifying, that the mountain wouldn't stop the bugs forever. I eased Susan a few inches away from me so that I could see her face as I spoke. Her eyes were puffy and red, and her face was wet from tears.

"Susan," I said gently. "We need you to come with us, down to my cabin. I can't leave you up here alone, and we can't defend both cabins as well as we can defend one."

"No-o-o," she cried painfully. "I can't just *leave*, Paul. Her soul is here! Her memories are here! Oh, my God, her scent is still probably on her pillow! Paul, what am I going to do without her?" She began crying that soul-tearing cry again.

"Susan. Susan, I'm begging you. I don't want to lose you, too. Please come with us. Phyllis will be so happy to see you, and so will the kids. Please."

After a couple more sobs, finally, Susan nodded. "I need to pack a few things first. Okay, Paul?"

"Sure, honey. We'll wait for you here."

She nodded, and slowly made her way back into the house. Once she had gently shut the front door behind her, I turned to the others.

"Gentlemen," I said quietly, "that was the hardest thing I've ever had to do."

Bobby came up and put a hand on my shoulder. "Paul, I've had to do that several times as a cop, and it never gets any easier."

We all sat, either on the porch steps, or the rocking chairs that decorated the porch. My mind was a whirl of things, flashing by at breakneck speeds.

Susan and Cheryl at our cabin for a picnic, Ralph throwing up blood and squirmers, barely escaping the city, getting Cheryl out of the cabin before she blew, being grateful for my wife and children....it all flashed through my head.

I can't say what the others were thinking, but they seemed as "checked out" as I was. They all had blank looks on their faces, and were staring at faraway places.

The shot made us all jump out of our reveries.

It had come from inside the cabin.

If my eyes were as wide as the other three sets, I looked very surprised. With me leading the way, we all burst into the cabin.

"Susan!" I yelled. "Susan!" When there was no answer, I told the others, "Look around down here! I'll look upstairs!"

I skipped a stair here and there as I ran up them. I threw open the master bedroom door.

I saw Susan.

She was sitting on the bed, sobbing quietly into her hands. A revolver was on the floor at her feet.

The relief I felt made my knees weak, and I almost lost my balance.

"I couldn't do it," Susan whispered. "I held the gun to my head, and squeezed the trigger. But something made me move the barrel away from my head. I couldn't do it." She buried her face in her hands and began crying quietly again.

I went over to her, and bent down to pick up the gun. I tucked it into my back waistband. I sat down beside the grieving woman, and pulled her close to me.

"Susan, please don't do that again," I whispered. "Cheryl wouldn't have wanted you to waste your life, just when the rest of us need you the most."

We rocked back and forth until Michael and Bobby came to the door. I nodded to them, and pulled Susan to her feet.

"Come on, sweetie," I said gently. "Let me help you pack a few things."

She wouldn't raise her eyes from the floor. But she nodded, and took my hand. Within a matter of minutes, we had her packed.

We headed back down the mountain.

PHYLLIS HAD THINGS going great when we got back to the cabin. She had a bucket line leading from the milk delivery van to the freezer outbuilding. They were moving butter and ice cream to the walk-in freezer. The milk was placed on the floor of the outbuilding, after all available space had been filled in the cabin's refrigerator. The ice chests that Michael and I had loaded had been filled, too.

Phyl saw us, and left Millie in charge of the brigade to come over to us. She hugged Susan, and took her over. Phyl smiled at me over Susan's shoulder, and I smiled back.

Richie wandered off to find Teresa.

The RV had brought two other kids with it, so, along with Keith and Clarissa, were all huddled together on the front porch.

"Well, I'd say this qualifies as the most stressful day ever," I said.

"You ain't kiddin', Paul," agreed Bobby.

"Did you guys register what Susan told us? That the creatures were all over the world?" asked Michael.

I nodded. "Yeah. I heard. Scares the shit out of me, too."

"What was it she said? That mountainous areas were too chilly for these bugs?" asked Bobby.

"This time of year, the average nighttime temperature is in the forties. I think I read somewhere that normal insects can't move around much in temperatures that low. Maybe that's what keeps them out of the mountains," I said.

"Well, that's great for now," said Bobby. "But what happens when the sun comes up, and the temperatures get warmer?"

"We'll have to cross that bridge when we get to it, I guess," I replied. "Meanwhile, you said you had an idea about all that stuff you brought, Bobby. What's your idea?"

"We build a moat," replied Bobby.

"A moat?" asked Michael.

"Yeah, I don't get it, either," I said.

"Here, I'll show you. Let me...oh, there's a good one," said Bobby. He walked a few steps away and picked up a stick. "Come over here to the light." He led the way over to the area directly in front of the milk truck's headlights and squatted down. He used the stick to draw a circle. "Okay, Paul, this is a circle surrounding our little haven here. If all of us pitch in and dig a good sized trench all the way around the area, we could shore up the sides with the wood. Dig the trench fairly deep, around a foot or so, and put the wood in so that it forms a 'V'. With that, we've formed a trough. Once we have that done, we pour concrete into the trough. It hardens, creating a moat all around the cabin and the outbuildings."

"Well, that's great, Bobby, but what good would it do? We could fill it with water, but that won't stop the bugs from just stepping...or flying...over it," I said.

Bobby shook his head and laughed. "We don't fill it with water, Paul"

"We fill it with gasoline," said Michael, matter-of-factly.

Bobby smiled and pointed at Michael. "Bingo! We fill it with gasoline when we know the bugs are coming. Then all it takes is one little match, and *poof*! We've got a barrier that no bug is going to cross."

I thought about it. It was a good plan. Mostly.

"What happens with the bugs that can fly?" I asked. "Won't they fly right over the trench?"

"Sure," said Bobby. "But we have flamethrowers for them. And if the juice in them runs low, maybe we can fabricate something with the gasoline and something that sparks. Like a flint, or something."

I thought about it. Not bad. Not bad at all. And we had to have something going to keep all of the idle hands going...something to work for that would protect everyone. I nodded, slowly at first, then faster. "Good plan, Bobby. We'll start tomorrow. We'll have to finish it soon, or the cement will harden inside the truck, and won't be any good to us at all. Or the ground will freeze solid. Yep, tomorrow it is. We'll tell everyone later. I only hope that we have enough digging tools."

Bobby smiled. "I covered that, too." He pointed to the police cruiser. "Inside are five picks, and five shovels, along with sledgehammers, regular hammers, nails, even a big roll of thick black plastic – the kind they use to landscape with. We can use that to line the wood and keep the concrete in place to harden."

"You're impressing me, Mr. Policeman," I said.

"Hey, protect and serve, Paul. Protect and serve."

Michael asked, "When are we going to tell everyone?"

I shrugged. "Why not now?"

Both Michael and Bobby nodded their agreement.

I stood up, and called everyone to gather around. Everyone came, and stood in a rough circle around the three of us.

"Bobby, here, came up with an idea for us to offer more protection for this place against the bugs. I'll let him explain."

Bobby explained the plan to everyone, and asked if there were questions. There weren't.

I took over. "So, we're going to start on this project first thing in the morning. We're also going to organize a rotating watch, to look out for bugs."

Ben, one of the men that came in the RV, said, "Hey, who made you the boss here?"

Voices in the group died down to silence. All were watching me, since I was the one that had been challenged.

Ha! Challenged! Already!

Quietly, I said, "I did. It's my cabin, Ben."

"It's my cabin, Ben," he said with a mocking voice. "Well, I just don't feel like digging dirt on your property, *Paul*. And I don't think I'm going to, either. Whatcha gonna do about it?" Ben stood with his hands on his hips, chest thrust out, playing the role of Big Billy Badass.

I was surprised how calm I was inside. I walked over to the man and looked into his eyes. "Then you go down the mountain."

Ben leaned over until our noses were an inch apart. He said, "Make me."

He hadn't noticed that my shotgun was barrel up, leaning toward him. The click, when I turned the safety off, was very loud in the yard.

"Trust me. You'll can leave on your own two feet, or you can be carried down the mountain," I said. "I won't risk lives to play nice."

In the light from the headlights, I could see a line of nervous sweat pop up across his forehead, and most of the color drained from his face. Slowly, very slowly, Ben leaned back, away from my face. The barrel of my shotgun followed him.

I raised my voice. "That goes for everyone! This place is not a democracy, this is my family's cabin! I'm more than happy to provide you with room and board, but safety is everyone's concern, and I'm the final say when it comes to that. Like some of your parents may have told you when you were teenagers – if you're under my roof, you'll play by my rules. If that's too much for you, then the road there also leads down."

I paused for emphasis. "Everyone, and I mean me, my wife, my kids, and *you*, will take turns digging, keeping watch, and assembling this trench tomorrow morning, beginning at seven." I turned to Ben and gave him a stern look. "I mean everyone, Ben. Even you."

He didn't like it. Oh, he didn't like it. But, he had no other choice. With a grim set to his lips, he nodded.

As I walked away with Bobby and Michael, Bobby said, "You're not done with him. You know that, right?"

"I know," I replied tonelessly.

PHYL AND I FINALLY got everyone bedded down. The children had their own rooms – boys in one and girls in the other. The two young people from McKelvie's were assigned to those rooms, too. That took up two of the three upstairs bedrooms.

The third upstairs bedroom was given to whoever wanted it. The same thing applied to the couch, love seat, and chairs in the living room. We didn't have enough pillows, but we had plenty of blankets, and the fire was kept warm.

Phyl and I had the master bedroom, and we shared it with Michael, Millie, Bobby, Billy, and Susan. They all had sleeping bags, provided by Michael, who had snuck them into the room early. They were part of the supplies he brought from the sporting goods store.

A couple of people that came in the RV chose to sleep there to alleviate some of the crowding in the cabin.

We arranged a watch schedule that had two people on duty at all times, for two hours for each watch shift. Phyl and I took the first watch. Bobby and his brother Billy would take the second, with Michael and Millie taking the third. Oddly enough, Richie and Teresa had volunteered for the last watch. They called themselves "the dawn patrol" and promised to wake us at six.

Phyl and I had settled down in the rocking chairs on the porch. I reached over to take her hand.

"It's been a rough day, hasn't it?" she said.

I smiled and nodded. "It sure has."

"How are you, Paul? How are you really?"

I thought for a minute. "Surprisingly, I'm okay. Maybe the shock is delayed, and hasn't sunk in yet, but, right now, I'm okay."

We rocked for a few minutes, comfortable with each other's company.

"Would you have shot that man if he hadn't backed away?"

Without hesitation, I said, "Yes."

We were silent for a few beats, and then she said, "I think you should have shot him anyway. He's only going to be trouble."

I sighed. "I know. But, I like to think that people are basically good, and want to help. I just want to give him his chance. If something happens later, then I'll boot him out."

Suddenly, a number of jets flew east over the mountain. The noise startled us as they passed over. By the time we had scrambled off of the porch, they were off in the distance. We could see the lights on at least three planes, and we saw what looked like missile contrails below them, reflected in the moonlight. Visibility from our position on the mountain was about twenty miles, so we were able to watch the contrails dip just below the horizon. We saw the flash of the explosions, and, a several seconds later, we could actually hear the pounding bass of their sound, almost like fireworks going off in the distance.

Phyl grabbed me when we saw the flash of the missiles, and held me tighter when the sound came to us.

I held her close, and reassured her. "They aren't nuclear. Just powerful missiles. We're safe."

We heard the front door close behind us. Bobby and Billy had come outside.

"The sound of the jets going over woke us. I hope you two don't mind if we join you," said Bobby.

"Yeah, can't fall asleep anyway," added Billy.

"Sure! The more, the merrier," I said.

I pointed off in the direction that the missiles had exploded, and explained what we had seen.

"Wow. So the military can still fight back. That's good news!" said Bobby.

"Maybe. As long as they don't use nukes, it's good news," I replied. "But I still think we're mostly on our own."

"You're probably right," agreed Bobby.

As we all watched, the jets passed over their target again, or, at least, we thought it was the jets. This time we didn't see any missiles. But we saw the flashes. The planes we saw were dropping bombs, and the flashes came fast and furious.

I wondered if all of that would have any effect on these creatures, and I said it out loud.

"Sure, it'll kill some...won't it?" pondered Billy.

"Oh, I hope so," said Phyllis. "I hate to think of what will happen if it doesn't."

"But killing some won't kill them all," said Bobby.

I sighed. "No. No, it won't. And I'm wondering if they've grown as large as they're going to get."

"Oh, now there's a worse thought! What if they grow to the size of elephants or something?" said Bobby.

"Or worse," said Billy.

"That's the trouble with genetically engineering things like those bugs," I said. "Unless you've really tested them out, you have no idea *what* surprises they have in store as they develop."

The four of us pondered that for a while as we watched the bombing of the creatures.

Bobby asked, "Paul, do you have satellite TV?"

"We do."

"I think we should be watching the news channels, if any are still broadcasting, and see if there's anything new that we should know about."

"He's right, Paul," said Phyllis.

"I think so, too, but the TV is in the living room. We'd wake up the entire house," I replied.

"What about the one in the bedroom?" asked Billy.

"Same thing," I said. "We'd wake Susan, or Michael, or Millie. Or all of them."

"Can you move the bedroom TV to your study?" asked Bobby. "No one is sleeping in there."

Phyllis looked at me, and nodded.

I said, "I believe we can, if the satellite cord will reach. If it won't, we can drill a hole through the bedroom wall. It's right next to the study. But, let's wait until tomorrow, okay? I don't want to wake everyone."

"Good enough. We can do that when we aren't digging," said Bobby.

We watched the bombing a bit longer, then Phyl and I went to bed.

Chapter 6

We rousted everyone out of bed at six-thirty. The elderly couple that owned the RV had the morning watch, and Phyllis, Millie, Teresa, and Clarissa were trying to put together some kind of breakfast for everyone. Susan was also in the kitchen area, trying to help out wherever she could.

Bobby and Billy had been busy little beavers during their watch. They had put down markers for the trench, noting places that had to be dug a little deeper than others so that the trench would remain mostly level. This was to keep the gasoline from pooling in lower levels at the expense of higher ground.

I hadn't thought of that. I'm glad Bobby had, and I said so.

"Not a big deal, Paul," Bobby said. "And the good part is that I think we'll have enough material left over to put one around Susan's cabin, too."

I looked at him. "Do you think that's necessary?"

"Maybe not urgent, but, yeah, Paul, I think it's necessary," Bobby replied. "It gives us a place to retreat to if we need it."

I thought about it for a moment. "It also gives us a place for overflow. I really don't think this will be all the people that we wind up with. Do you?"

Bobby shook his head. "Honestly? I don't know. I do know that the bugs will really be active today, and they may very well decide to brave the rarified air here. I think we should get started on the ditch." He and Billy began walking toward the cabin. "Bill and I are going to grab a bite of breakfast and get started. Will you send us some help soon?"

"Sure. As soon as I can."

I turned to go talk to some of the other people, and found myself face-to-face with Ben.

"Good morning, Ben," I said.

Ben looked surprised that I had spoken to him with civility. "Good morning."

"Listen, Ben, I'm willing to let bygones be bygones. Yesterday was a shock to everyone. Why don't we start over?"

Ben shook his head. "No. Sorry. I'll be leaving today."

With concern, I replied, "Ben, you don't really want to go down the mountain. Stay here with us. It's safer."

"I'm not going down the mountain," he said. "I'm going up and over the mountain. There's bound to be others that I can join up with. I just wanted to know if I could have enough food and water for a week or so."

I looked at his face. "It may not be safe."

Ben shrugged. "I don't care."

Quietly, I said to him, "Would it help if I apologized to you publicly? So everyone can hear? I'll do it, if you'll stay with us."

Ben looked as if he wanted to say yes, but he let his pride do the talking. "No. I'll be leaving within the hour, Stiles, with or without the supplies."

I shook my head at his obstinate behavior. I knew that no argument would penetrate his pride. I looked him in the eyes and said, "Of course you can have the supplies, Ben, but I wish you'd reconsider."

Ben nodded once to me and said, "Thanks. Good luck to you."

"And to you."

With that, we walked to the freezer building, and loaded him up. He had milk, several cans of various soup, fruit, and vegetables, several bottles of water, and some crackers. I gave him a sleeping bag, and a backpack. I also gave him a snub-nosed .38 revolver and a box of ammunition. He had been alone when Bobby found him, and he would be leaving our camp alone, for a lonely, torturous trek up the mountain to the top, then over to the other side. I'd never made that climb, but Susan had. She and Cheryl had done it only once, because there were nothing but more steep mountains on the other side. I shared this information with Ben, and gave him what directions I remembered from Susan's account of the trip. He left, without a single look back.

I said a silent prayer for his safety from the bugs, and went inside to have breakfast and to share the news.

TWO HOURS LATER, I was swinging a pick with five other people, and five more were using shovels to move the dirt that us "pickers" had loosened. It was hard, backbreaking labor, and my muscles were really singing the blues, but I kept at it. By the time my shift ended an hour later, I could barely straighten out my hands. But, we had made some serious progress – three-fourths of the trench had been built. Bobby had assigned people to begin putting down the lumber, forming the Vs that would support the concrete in the trench. Once a portion of the trench was lined with lumber, a few more people began lining the trench with the black plastic. At the rate we were going, we'd be pouring concrete by lunch.

I had turned on the big TV in the main room of the cabin. Not much was coming across the satellite, but we did find an all-news channel. The bugs were now all over the world, with the exception of extreme northern countries, Australia, and New Zealand. Planes had been attacked by swarms of flying creatures, much like the ones we had encountered inside McKelvie's, and caused most of those planes to crash. Most governments in the affected countries had gone underground to their protective bunkers, but, unless they were airtight, they were vulnerable to bug attacks. The all-new channel that I had found was also in an underground location, but they didn't say where. I assigned the elderly couple, Lee and Bernice Adams, the task of keeping up with the reports on TV and making notes of everything that seemed relevant.

Killing the creatures was an easy thing, but the enormous numbers made it a difficult task. They kept hatching new bugs to replace the dead ones. The dead ones were food and shelter for eggs, especially the squirmers, and with their fast growth, killing a city full of them would only last a day or so.

The bugs were rapidly killing off mankind.

They had learned quickly, and began attacking military units that got close to them. The bugs were very good at ripping apart tanks and other armored equipment. I guess they had figured out that a tasty morsel could be found at the center of those large metal beasts. Or a hatchery. Either way, humans were being eliminated with an alarming regularity.

Richie took my pick, and began his shift. I told him to be damn careful, because I didn't want to have to sew his foot back on. My sewing skills were limited.

I stiffly walked over to the cabin, and went inside. I wanted to sit down in the worst way, but I needed water. I said hello to Lee and Bernice, and headed for the kitchen area. Phyllis was doing her two hour tour with the shovel, so I helped myself to the water. At least our well was deep, clear, and clean. I drank water until I sloshed, and went back into the living room.

"Anything new?" I asked Lee.

Lee looked at his notes. "Well, the bugs are all over the Middle East. Silly bastards that let them loose are being eaten alive." He snickered. "I hope that every one of their seventy-two virgins are male!" He snickered again, and Bernice hit him on the arm. "Ow!"

"You know better than that, old man," scolded Bernice.

Lee continued. "The reason that the bugs are winning is that they don't have any natural predators. They're too big for any animals that are live today. The only kind challenge they have of any kind is man, and they're making short work of us. The TV still says that the mountains are the safest places on earth right now."

"Good. Let's hope it stays that way," I said. I went over to one of the chairs and collapsed into it. My eyes were drawn to the screen.

Lee had muted the sound when I came inside. The TV had been displaying video feeds from around the world, and the carnage was horrible, and the destruction was mostly complete. As I watched, the haggard-looking news anchor came onscreen. Over his shoulder was a superimposed image of a bug beside a city bus.

"Oh, my God," I said. "Lee! Turn that up!"

Lee scrambled for the remote, pressed the button, and brought back the sound.

"...and the bugs have grown tremendously. Some have grown as large as a city bus, and have huge jaws capable of biting an adult in half, or swallowing a child whole. We take you to video captured earlier, and we warn you that it is graphic."

The picture cut to a millipede-type bug pushing over a city bus, tearing it open, and ripping people to shreds.

"May God have mercy on us all," said Bernice quietly.

I STUMBLED BACK OUTSIDE to the dig site. Almost everyone was there, or close by. Phyllis saw my face, and told everyone to stop.

When I got close enough, I told them what had just been on TV, and that the bugs were only getting larger.

To punctuate my words, the sound of planes came again from overhead. We looked up in time to see several high flying fighters fly over the mountain.

"Looks like the military is bombing the bugs again. I pray to God that they don't use nukes on them. Not on our own country," I said.

"Should we keep digging?" asked the gasoline truck driver – Mitch, I think his name was.

I nodded. "Yeah. We still need to protect ourselves from the bugs. The bombs won't kill them all."

I sank down to sit on the ground. I was shell-shocked. Some idiot in Russia created these things for some Islamic terrorist group, and didn't give a thought to how the creatures would change, or breed, or grow. The only thought was for the money...not for people. Probably the silly Islamic extremists were dead by now, and the Russian scientists that created the bugs were probably dead, too, because the bugs didn't care about religion, or money. Just food.

The sad thing was that if they had just worried about their own business, the damn bugs would never have been created.

We never did hear any explosions or see any bright flashes. But I was sure that the high-flying planes had found targets somewhere. There seemed to be plenty to go around.

We did finish getting the trench ready by lunchtime. We poured the concrete after lunch, and made sure that the trough was formed properly. After that, all we had to do was wait for the concrete to dry.

We had enough materials to build a trench around Susan's cabin. We made plans to start on that the next morning.

Later that afternoon, I was inside the cabin, checking to see if any channels besides the all-news channel were broadcasting. A Mexican channel, and a channel that specialized in religious programming were all that I could find. Both continued to fade in and out, and I had the distinct impression that they were being broadcast with automation, because they both began rebroadcasting the same programming after a few hours. I changed the TV back to the all-news channel, and muted the sound. I could hear the children playing outside.

Suddenly, I heard Keith yelling. "Dad! *DAD!*" I dropped the remote, picked up my shotgun, and ran outside to see what was wrong.

Keith was standing with Clarissa and the other children in the middle of the front yard. I scanned the area as I ran to them, but I didn't see anything threatening.

I stopped, and put my hand on Keith's shoulder. "What's wrong, son?"

"Listen!"

I began listening. At first, it didn't register, because it was in the low background. But, as it got louder, it registered. It was a vehicle engine, and it was struggling to get up the mountain on our steep road! From the sound, it would be at the cabin soon.

I turned to Keith and the other children. "Go get Bobby, Billy, and Michael. Richie too, if he wants to come. Then, I want you four to go hide behind the well house until we know if they're friendly or not. Now, scram!" I shooed the kids away.

As they scrambled off to find the guys, I focused on the sound again. Now, it sounded like two vehicles, but I couldn't make out what kind of vehicles they might be.

The guys must have been close, because they suddenly were right there, and all had shotguns.

"Hear that?" I asked. "Sounds like more than one, doesn't it?"

Bobby nodded grimly. "Sounds like one of them is a city bus. A big diesel bus."

Now that he had pointed it out, I agreed. It did sound like a bus.

We didn't have long to wonder. As we waited, the two vehicles turned the curve on the road, and came into sight. One of the vehicles was a city bus – Bobby had been right about that. The second vehicle was an ambulance. It followed the bus closely. The windows on the bus were all down, and people suddenly started staring out. They shouted to the bus driver to stop, and the bus came to a stop directly in front of us. The ambulance hung back a little bit...maybe being wary until they knew our intentions.

Bobby was still wearing his uniform – none of my clothes fit him, and he hadn't hunted around much to find anything else. He waved to the bus, then to the ambulance. I waved, too. Maybe the others did, I don't know for sure. They were behind me.

The doors slid open on the bus, and a uniformed lady got off of the bus. Obviously, she was the driver.

"Oh, praise God! Praise Jesus! Thank you, Lord, for leading us here!" she was repeating over and over. When she got to Bobby, she wrapped him in her massive arms and hugged him. "Oh, man, you is a sight for sore eyes! My name's Latisha and I drove that bus all the way here from the city! I got a busload of people, and I got a for-real doctor back in that ambulance! Can you make room for us? Is it safe here? I got kids, too...and medicine."

I laughed and held out my hand to her. "Latisha, I'm Paul Stiles. This is my cabin, and you folks are more than welcome to stay, with one condition: we all work to stay safe here. If that's okay, you're all welcome here."

Latisha waved her hand at me. "Oh, shoot, don't be silly, Mr. Stiles! We expect to keep thangs safe! We ain't fools." She turned toward the bus. "Okay, people, come on out! It's safe! We got a place to stay!"

From the shadows inside the bus, three men descended the bus steps in single file. Each of them had what looked like semiautomatic rifles, with extra-round magazines. We would have lasted less than a minute, if we had been threats.

I threw back my head and laugh a long and hearty laugh. Soon, we all were laughing at the absurdity of the situation. All of us, aiming our guns, waiting to kill each other, when the bugs would probably take care of that for us. If not this fall, then next spring for sure.

When we were through laughing, I told Latisha to let us put some planks down so that they could cross the trench, and that they could park the vehicles as close to the cabin as possible.

Chapter 7

Thirty-three more souls joined us that day, bringing our total to sixty-one. Their story was no different than ours. They barely made it out of the city, and had joined the long lines of traffic heading to the mountains.

Latisha said that they had taken our road in the hope of finding a way over the mountain. When I told her that the road ended at the other cabin, she started laughing.

"Praise God that he led us here, then," she said. "I believe He brought us here for a reason."

They had spent the night inside a concrete block garage in Pine Valley, and it was only luck that had spared that town from the invasion.

"But, when we left, we could hear the buzzing of some of the flying things over on the east side of town. We vamoosed just as fast as that bus would go," said Latisha.

The doctor was indeed a "for-real" doctor. His name was Jeremiah Case, and he had traveled in the ambulance with two paramedics. Dr. Case had worked as an ER doctor in Pine Valley. The paramedics were from the city. The passengers ran the gamut of people of all ages. The guns had been picked up at a sporting goods store in Pine Valley, and some of the passengers knew how to use them. One of those, Roger Tippet, was an ex-Marine that had seen action in Iraq.

As we were all getting acquainted, Lee Adams called to me.

"Paul! You might want to come see this on TV!" he yelled.

I waved to him, and invited anyone else that wanted to come and watch to feel free to come in.

As some of us got to the front door, Lee said, "The newsman said that bugs were trying to get into their studio. They're underground, but they don't think they can hold out. He said the bugs had come in through the ventilation shafts."

"Oh, crap," I said.

Almost everyone was inside, watching the nervous, sweating news anchor.

"...and the situation is grim, folks. We hope we've given you enough information to survive, but, as we can see, that may not be enough. The creatures are tenacious, strong, and hungry. We can hear them in the shafts, and they're nibbling at the bunker doors. I don't think we have much time. It's been a pleasure reporting the news to you, and I thank you for your viewership. We're going to turn the camera upward, so that you won't have to watch us die. Goodbye, and good luck."

With those words, the camera panned up to the bunker ceiling, and all that was left was sound. We could hear lots of shouting, tearing metal, pounding, and then, finally, screams. I turned the television off.

"That's enough of that," I said. "Bless them, and I hope the end came quickly for them."

Latisha had bowed her head, and was saying a quiet prayer for the people in the newsroom. When her prayer was through, we all said, "Amen."

DR. CASE ASKED IF HE could set up a small examination room in one of the rooms upstairs. I said that he could use the study, and that we'd move everything out, if he needed us to. He did, with the exception of the desk and chair.

The good doctor said that he and the paramedics would be on hand for anything that required medical attention. I told him that I hoped no one would need his services.

"I already have someone that needs my services," said Dr. Case.

"Oh, really? What's the problem?" I asked.

"It's one of the passengers that came from the city with Latisha. I've never seen anything like it," he finished.

I leaned against the desk. "Doc, I have to be honest with you. I'm afraid of a bug infection here. We've been lucky." I explained to him about our encounter with Cheryl, and what happened with Ralph.

"That's interesting. Have you ever seen the full incubation period for an infection? Do you know what the beginning looks like? Or how long it takes from infection to this 'empty eyes' condition you described?"

I shook my head. "No, Doc, I can't say that I have. For all I know, all of us could be infected, and we'd never know it, until we all threw up blood and squirmers."

"That's information that I don't have. Can you describe what you're talking about? In detail? It may help me help others."

So I did. The empty, milky eyes. The ability to stay mobile, even thought their minds and body were being devoured on the inside. The final attempt to speak, then bending at the waist and throwing up their life blood, mixed in with fast-growing squirmers.

"Come to think of it, Doc, I don't even know what kind of bugs the squirmers grow into, except by inference. That came from the bug that came through the sewer lines at my home."

"I would imagine that the reproduction is much the same, no matter what kind of bug happens to form." Dr. Case ran his hands through his hair. "How could someone be so short-sighted? How could someone genetically create like this without any thought as to the outcome, or the ramifications?"

"Some people just hate the U. S. that badly, I guess. They probably thought they were some kind of martyrs or heroes or something." I paused a moment. "So, tell me about your patient."

Dr. Case looked at me. "I'm not sure that I can, with doctor-patient privacy."

"I think that's over with, Doc," I said. "I have to know what kind of threat this person is to all of us."

"Why? So you can torch him?" he said sharply. Immediately, he said, "I'm sorry. I understand how hard that was for you, and I understand why you had to do it."

I chose not to get angry. But, I reserved the right. "Point taken, Doc. And, make no mistake about it – I will do it again, if I have to. I have to keep the group safe, and that's all there is to it."

Dr. Case looked at the floor, studying the problem. "Okay. You're right, of course." He took a deep breath. "The patient was penetrated by a 'squirmer', as you call them."

I felt my eyes widening. "Doc, that's very bad!"

"Maybe not, Paul," he replied. "I was there when it happened, and I took several precautions. I caught the thing with tiny forceps, and I believe I pulled most of it out of my patient, but I couldn't be sure. Then, I doused the area with both alcohol and peroxide, and gave the man an injection of antibiotics, anti-viral, and...well...praziquantel."

"What is praziquantel?"

Dr. Case lightly smiled. "Worm medicine."

"*Worm* medicine?" I asked incredulously.

"It's used primarily for treatment of tapeworms. It seems to have worked so far. He was infected two days ago, about the time your neighbor was throwing up on your lawn mower."

I couldn't get over it. Worm medicine. But, then again, I could see why. And if it worked, so much the better.

I thought of something. "But, we don't know the incubation period, do we?"

Dr. Case shook his head. "No."

"So he could still be infected?"

"Yes."

"Then we really should quarantine him...at least for another week."

"Sure," said Case. "Where do you want to put him? Your room? My room? The bus, where many people sleep? Or we could put him in the outbuilding with the freezer."

I held my hand up. "I get your point, Doc." I thought for a minute. "Okay, as long as he has someone with him at all times."

"That's right along my line of thinking."

And that was that. At least for the possibly infected patient.

LATE THAT AFTERNOON, I was checking the batteries inside the outbuilding. Our output was holding up well, and it looked as if we had enough solar power and wind to keep them fully charged. I was checking a few line connections, when Bobby stepped into the building.

"Paul, can you step outside here just for a minute?" he asked.

"Sure." I picked up my shotgun, which was always with me now, and stepped outside. "What is it?"

"Listen," said Bobby.

I listened. I heard the wind and nothing else...at first. Slowly, I began to pick up light sounds, sort of like the far-off buzz of a chainsaw.

"Is that a chainsaw that I'm hearing?" I asked.

"I'm not sure," said Bobby. "I listened to it for a few minutes before I came to get you, but I couldn't decide what it was. I thought that two sets of ears were better than one."

I listened for a bit more, but the sound had drifted away, and was gone.

The sun was almost down, so I shrugged and said, "I guess whoever it was gave up for the day."

Bobby had a concerned look on his face. "Maybe. Yeah, maybe you're right."

Honestly, I forgot about it. We were so busy that night arranging the watch with the extra people, and scheduling people to go to Susan's cabin the next morning to build a trench, that I didn't give the chainsaws another thought.

But I thought of it the next day. I thought of it big time.

BOBBY AND BILLY HAD taken over the construction of the trench at Susan's. The two brothers took their work crews along the road that curved and meandered along the side of the mountain up to Susan's cabin. Past Susan's cabin, the road became a dirt track, used mostly by hunters and four-wheeler enthusiasts.

I stayed behind at the cabin, mostly checking the emergency generators, organizing and storing the supplies, and making sure our supply of weapons were clean, oiled, and functioning. I set up shop in the front yard, with Phyllis and Latisha giving me a hand with the job.

It was a warm day for late September. The temperatures were in the mid-70s, and the sun was shining brightly.

Soon, Phyllis left to go inside. She, along with Susan, would be putting together something for lunch. Michael, who had also stayed behind that day, sat down and took Phyl's place.

The three of us were enjoying the day, and were getting to know each other.

"Paul, what happened to you in the city?" asked Latisha.

"We barely made it out of our house," I replied. I told her and Michael all about that morning, and how we barely made it out of the driveway. "If the sun hadn't been shining, that thing hiding under the lawn mower would have gotten at least one of us."

Tyrese, one of the passengers on Latisha's bus, came into the front yard with Richie during my story, and sat down to listen.

"What about you, Michael?" asked Latisha.

Michael told them about not knowing anything about the bugs until I came into the store, and what had happened with the lone customer in front, and the flying things inside McKelvie's.

"Man. McKelvie's," marveled Latisha. She looked at Richie, then pointed at him in recognition. "Yeah, I remember you! You always so nice to ever'body! And there was a nice little girl that ran the register, too, when I went in...a thin little blonde girl..."

"That must have been Teresa," said Richie. "Mr. Stiles got her out, too. She's her, and so is Millie."

"*Millie?* That *rascal!* How come I ain't seen her yet?"

"I don't know, ma'am," said Richie.

"I think it was because you got here so late yesterday evening," I said. "By the time we got everyone fed, and found a place to sleep, it was time to *go* to sleep."

Latisha laughed hard at that. "You right, honey! I jus' barely remember you and them two Barnes boys!"

"How about you, Latisha?" asked Michael. "How did you get out of the city?"

The smile came off of her face as if a switch had been thrown. "I ain't told it all, so ya'll gonna have to bear with me. I'm liable to cry while I'm tellin' it, so ya'll don't laugh, you hear?"

I reached over and squeezed her shoulder. "Not a chance, Latisha. We've all seen things that we'd rather have forgotten."

Latisha looked at the ground and said, "Yeah, I guess you're right." She lifted her head and stared at the horizon. "I just wonder, though."

"Wonder what?" asked Michael.

"I just wonder if this is God's Judgment Day."

Of course, none of us had an answer for that.

Latisha took a deep breath. "Okay, you asked for it. Here's the story of one bus driver."

Chapter 8

"I wasn't even sposed to be drivin' that day," said Latisha. "It was my day off, but so many had called in that my supervisor promised me an extra day off the next week, on Friday...plus time and a half for a full shift, if I'd just come in and drive for a few hours. Hey, I got four kids, all teenagers...I could sure use the money!

"Well, I went in, and had to drive this old-ass bus that didn't have no accordion in the middle. Just a stiff, old, city bus. The route was different than my own, but I already knew that was gonna happen. So, I ran through my checklist and got started.

"My route was in the east part of the city."

My eyes widened. "Oh, crap." I said.

Latisha shook her head. "I didn't see nothing at first. People got on and off like ususal. Some of 'em looked kinda weird, but that's life in the city, ain't it? People always be lookin' weird."

I noticed that Latisha had been folding and refolding her cleaning cloth several times, and wouldn't look at us.

"I got a bad habit when I'm drivin' the route," she continued. "I don't always notice everybody that gets on the bus. I mean, I don't look at 'em. I just keep my eyes focused on traffic around me, and I don't watch the people. I wasn't on my usual route, so I just didn't feel like socializin' that day. So, I didn't see her when she got on the bus. I mean, I *saw* her, but I didn't look at her, you know what I mean?

"Tyrese, who was it that told me about her? Was it Manuel?" asked Latisha.

Tyrese nodded. "I think it was, Latisha."

Latisha nodded. "I think so, too." Unfolded and folded went the cleaning cloth. "Manuel came up front and told me that there was a really sick lady on the bus. God help me, I said somethin' smart-assed, like 'what I look like, a nurse?'" A tear welled up and ran down her cheek. "At the next stop, everybody had started hollerin' that she was sick, and she needed help. The bus was stopped, so I stood up, intendin' to read them all the riot act. Then I saw her."

Latisha unfolded and folded the cloth again, and wiped a tear from her cheek with the back of her hand. "She had this long, stringy black hair that looked like it hadn't been washed in a couple of days. Her skin was pale, and her eyes were milky and empty, just like you said your neighbor had, Paul."

She raised her head and stared off at the horizon. "I told her to get off the bus. Instead of callin' for help, I told her to get off my damn bus. Awwww, *God!*" she wailed, and burst into tears.

I reached over and squeezed her shoulder after a moment. "Latisha, you couldn't have helped her at that point. She was already gone."

"But I didn't know that then!" she yelled. "That's the *point*, Paul! Instead of tryin' to help that poor woman, I just couldn't be troubled with her! I told her to get off the *bus* like she was *nuthin'!"*

She sobbed and cried a little more. When she calmed down, she started talking again.

"People thought I was heartless, and the woman walked slowly to the doors in the front of the bus. A man got off with her. He had one hand on the small of her back, and was holding her arm with the other. They got about two steps away from the bus when the woman did what you said your neighbor did. She threw up a gallon of blood, with this black *goo* mixed in with it. It got all over that man that got off with her. Then she threw up again, and laid down on the sidewalk, all curled up. All of us were just staring out the windows at them, and suddenly the man starts slapping at himself all over, like he was gettin' attacked by a swarm of mosquitos. He finally took off running down the street. I shut the doors and took off away from there. I had seen them squirmin' things in the crap she threw up, and I saw the ones that landed on that man. I wasn't gonna stick around for no more. I radioed in to dispatch and told them what was goin' on, and they told me to come back in, that it was happenin' all over the city. I yelled at everybody that we were heading back to the main station, and that everyone would be taken wherever they wanted to go, but it was an emergency situation, and that was that. We started back, and if we saw one, we saw a dozen of those empty-eyed people wandering the sidewalks within just a couple of blocks. A couple of them threw up as we drove by.

"After about four blocks, we saw our first bug."

"See, we di'n't know at the time, but Latisha saved us all when she made that sick chick get off the bus," said Tyrese. "If that chick had thrown up on the bus, we'da all been eat by now." He laughed. It was a low and throaty sound. "Woman saved all our asses, and we be callin' her a hunnert differ'n't kinds of bitch!" His face turned serious again. "She right. That first bug, it was about the size of a cocker spaniel...looked like a big centipede, but it had a long snout, with teeth. And it was all furry on its body, kinda red, like fox fur. Thing crossed the street ahead of us, chasin' some wino. Thing caught the wino, knocked it right the fuck down, man! Then it bit his head off. Latisha jus' kep' drivin'. Few blocks later, we passed a big bunch of flyin' bugs, like you guys talked about in the grocery store. They knocked down three people that we know of, and ripped 'em apart. Couple of 'em hit the bus, but jus' left a dent in the roof."

"Wasn't nobody callin' me names after that, praise God," said Latisha. "Mostly, it was 'hurry up' or 'don't stop' I was hearin' then." She had resumed folding and unfolding the cleaning cloth. Then she looked at the horizon again. "God forgive me, but I ran over a couple of empty-eyed people. And a lot of bugs. Sunlight wasn't stoppin' these bad boys, Paul. You don't realize the confusion that it was – people runnin' everywhere, bugs chomping down or layin' eggs in 'em, bugs runnin' around everywhere, cars drivin' every which way...it was crazy on the east side, gentlemen." Unfold. Fold. "We stayed off the freeway. Every time we came close to an on-ramp, we could see how packed it was. Cars weren't movin' at all, and it wasn't because of traffic. It was because of the bugs! They were everywhere!"

A Hispanic man, one of Latisha's passengers, Pablo, I think, had come up to us during Latisha's last few sentences. He offered a couple of comments.

"Latisha kept driving. Didn't matter what got in front of that bus, Latisha kept driving. She saved us all."

Fold. Unfold. "The bugs started getting fewer and fewer the farther west we traveled," she said. "It's a good thing, too, or we wouldn't have made it."

"Couple of dudes turned on some radio," added Tyrese. "Said that the mountains was the safest place to be."

"So that where we headed," said Latisha. "We hit Pine Valley right about dark-thirty, and decided to take a chance on gettin' some sleep there, and keep truckin' in the mornin'. We found this old-lookin' gas station, with a two-bay garage. Wasn't nobody there, so we parked the bus inside, closed the doors, and sealed ourselves in."

Pablo said, "Some of us left, though. We had to have weapons...food. So we took a chance on leaving the gas station."

"Good thing they did, too," said Tyrese. "We hit a pawn shop that somebody had left open. Had a hidden room in the back. That's where we found the machine guns."

"We gathered as much as we could carry, and took them back to the garage. Then, we went out again for food," continued Pablo. "The market was empty, too. Everybody had just left, but didn't take anything with them!"

"So, we scored with the food, too, man," said Tyrese. "Took three trips, and lots of creative storage, but we got a lot in the bus."

"How did you meet Dr. Case?" asked Michael.

"Pure, dumb luck," said Tyrese.

Latisha actually laughed. "Him and the two paramedics came screamin' into the gas station parkin' lot with that ambulance, leavin' skid marks everywhere, they stopped so fast! They all three came bustin' outta that thing like their hair was on fire and their asses was catchin'!"

"Why did they come out of the ambulance like that?" I asked.

"It was because of Manuel," said Latisha. "A squirmer was in the back with him..."

I interrupted her, since I could guess that Manuel was the one Dr. Case had told me about. "Say no more! I wouldn't want to be around a squirmer, either, if I didn't have to be!" I didn't want word circulating about Manuel's near-infection. I wanted to keep that to myself for the time being.

Latisha seemed to sense that, and didn't finish the story. "So, to make a long story short, they joined up with us. This mornin', we started up this hill, and we was determined to find us a hole somewhere to get into, and pull the door in behind us. And, sure 'nuff, we found you folks." Unfold. Fold. "I just hope God finds it in his mercy to forgive me throwing that woman off the bus that way, and for running over them other empty-eyed people."

Faintly, in the distance, I heard the chainsaw that Bobby and I had heard late the day before. It faded in and out, as if caught by the wind and spread out along the mountain.

"You guys hear that?" I asked.

Everyone stopped to listen.

"Sounds like a chainsaw," said Richie.

"It could be one of them model airplanes that runs by radio control or somethin," said Tyrese.

The sound gradually got louder.

"I don't think that's a model airplane. Or a chainsaw," said Michael.

We listened a little bit longer. Finally, I couldn't take the not knowing.

"Let's load up, people," I said.

Each of us took a weapon and loaded it. We began watching all around us, waiting to see what would come out of the trees. Whatever was making that buzzing noise, we all knew it wasn't made by humans.

As we watched, Susan opened the door of the cabin and called out. "Lunch is ready! Come and get it!"

At the end of Susan's sentence, the source of the noise burst over the trees on the north side. It was shaped like a wasp, with long black wings and a thin abdomen. That was the best of the resemblance, however. It had the one long antenna that all of the bugs had, but this thing had a long, almost canine snout, with many teeth and a long tongue. Its fur was black and yellow, like a hornet, and it had eight legs. Each leg ended in what could be called paws, and each paw had retractable claws at the end of each of the five toes. Each claw looked very sharp. Its eyes were not multi-faceted like you would expect on an insect. Instead, they were black, emotionless and empty, and resembled the eyes of a reptile. The beast was at least seven feet long.

A fast though ran through my mind – it was a curse upon the scientist whose imagination cooked up this beast.

Susan screamed from the front porch. I fired my shotgun and apparently missed the thing completely. It began zig-zagging around, much like a fly will when it's swatted at with a swatter. Latisha and Michael fired, and both missed. Richie fired the .38 revolver he held, and managed to scratch the creature, because its buzzing became louder and angrier.

And it screamed.

Later, we all decided that a scream was what we heard. It was a high-pitched screech, emitted from its snout. We continued firing, and it continued evading the shots. It began zooming in and out toward the group of us on the front lawn, and we all had to duck a couple of times.

Meanwhile, Susan, Phyllis, and a couple of others had opened fire from the porch. Both women were using rifles, and both tagged the creature by leading it a little. It screamed again, a long, piercing howl, seemingly from pain. The creature was bleeding, and its blood was a dark, maroon color. It screamed once more, then landed on the front lawn about fifty feet away from us.

Once it landed, Tyrese opened fire on the creature with his machine pistol. He peppered a thirty-round burst all along its side, while the rest of us also opened fire. Soon, the flying beast was only a bloody carcass, mutilated by our weapons.

We stood silent, staring at the monster.

Tyrese broke the silence. "God-*damn!* I thought the damn mountains was supposed to be *safe!*"

Latisha put her hand on his shoulder. "Calm down, Tyrese. It's over now."

But it wasn't.

We heard a huge buzzing noise coming from the same direction as the first beast. Over the top of the trees, five more streamed into the sky over the front yard.

These five creatures were at least twice as massive as the first one. If these were any indication, we had apparently killed a young creature. And, if we had killed their young, they were going to be a little upset.

"Holy shit!" I screamed. "Shoot! Shoot at them! Get to the house! Get going! Run!"

It's very hard to accurately fire a weapon while running for your life. The best you can hope for is that one shot get lucky. We weren't lucky.

One of the flying beasts swooped, and knocked Pablo to the ground. Pablo screamed. A second beast landed on top of Pablo, and dug its claws into his back. It curled its lower abdomen exactly as a wasp does, and it impaled Pablo with a foot-long stinger that was as big around as a human arm. It hit Pablo twice more before Tyrese dropped to his knees and started firing his machine pistol. There were only twenty or so rounds left in the magazine. He wounded the beast, and shot off one of its wings, but it wasn't enough to kill it. Wounded, it could not fly, but it detached its claws from Pablo, and tried to limp away.

The rest of us had reached the porch as the four flying beasts zipped around the front yard, trying to protect their wounded comrade. Tyrese slapped a new magazine into the machine pistol and was ready to open fire again. He was too late. One of the beasts hit him from behind. The machine pistol went flying away from Tyrese. The man's face was a rictus of pain, and, as we all watched, the creature lifted Tyrese off of the ground and began to fly away with him, like a spider caught by a wasp.

We shot at the beast, but not much. We were afraid of hitting Tyrese. While we were watching Tyrese being carried away, a second creature had allowed the wounded one to grasp with its claws, and they flew away. A third creature carried the young one.

Pablo lay dead in the front yard as the creatures returned to their hideaway.

LATE THAT AFTERNOON, we buried Pablo at the edge of the trees, alongside Cheryl. We had incinerated Pablo's body just in case that stinger had also laid eggs. Latisha said a few words over our fallen comrade, and led us in prayer.

When she was through, I said, "Meeting. Everyone. Inside."

Once everyone was inside, with sentries on the front porch and on the back porch, I began saying what I wanted to say.

"Has anyone seen any more planes today?" I asked. General silence. "Okay, has anyone tried listening to a radio?" General silence. "Has anyone used a cell phone?" I knew the answer to that – almost everyone raised a hand. "Anyone had luck? I know the service is available from the tower, but has anyone spoken with someone outside of our group?" General silence again.

"What are you saying, Paul?" asked Bobby.

I took a breath. "I'm thinking we're on our own. I don't think any organized help is coming, and I truly believe that we're going to have to help ourselves."

There were general murmurs of agreement.

"Those flying things obviously have a nest close by, somewhere here in the mountains. What do you think we should do about it?"

"Do you think they'll be back?" someone asked. I couldn't see who it was.

"Of course they'll be back," I said. "We killed one of them, and wounded another. They carried Tyrese off as either a snack or a place to lay eggs. When they find out we're easy pickings, they'll be back. And I don't think this cabin will hold up in a full-scale bug attack." I looked at a few faces. "So, again, what do you think we should do about it?"

"What do you want us to say, Paul?" asked one of the paramedics. "We're all scared to death of those things, but we aren't safe here while they're around."

"You want us to hunt down their nest, don't you?" asked Billy Barnes.

Everyone was staring at me. Finally, I nodded. "Yeah. I do. I think we should take the flamethrowers, find their nest, and burn them out."

Richie was shaking his head. "No. No. Not me. Did you see how big those things are? And that's just the ones we *saw*! No. Count me out. Uh-uh."

"One other thing we have to consider," said Bobby Barnes. "The mountains were supposed to be safe, according to the last government broadcast, because the temperatures were too cool here for the bugs." He looked around. "What if those things aren't the only creatures to have made their homes in these mountains? We need information about why those things are here."

"We know that these creatures have lungs," said Dr. Case. "We heard that in the police dispatches that we received. I have a theory that many of these bugs contain mammal characteristics...including being warm-blooded."

"What does this 'warm-blooded' mean?" asked Manuel.

Dr. Case answered. "It means that these bugs generate their own heat. And if they can generate their own heat, they can live in colder temperatures, if shelter is available." He crossed his arms and put a finger across his chin. "If I had a specimen, I could perform an autopsy on it. Dissect it, to see if my guess is correct."

"And may the good Lord have mercy on us if Dr. Case proves what he's sayin'," said Latisha.

Several murmurs of "Amen" came from around the main floor of the cabin.

I spoke up. "I guess it's settled, then. We'll send out a search-and-destroy team tomorrow in the direction that those things flew. Maybe we'll get lucky and find the nest."

Someone in the crowd said, "More likely you'll get eaten by the nest."

"Maybe so, but it's a risk we have to take. Michael, are those walkie-talkie radios still in good working order?" I asked.

"They are!" he affirmed.

"Good. Who wants to go with me?" I asked.

"You're not going, Paul," said Bobby.

Silence ran rampant in the room.

"Excuse me?" I asked.

"You're the group leader. You're responsible for everyone. You are staying here, and I will hear no argument about it."

"Now, wait a minute...!" I began.

"*No,* Paul. If the search-and-destroy group turns into the Tuesday Night Bug Snack Group, then the group leader will still be available to plan the second attack. You're too valuable to the group to take a risk like that," said Bobby.

I looked around the room. "Is that how everyone feels?"

A resounding "Yes!" came from all around the room.

Bobby looked at me and winked. "I'll take four people. I want Nick, Manuel, Michael, and Susan. Anyone have objections?" Nick was the driver of the gasoline tanker.

There were no objections.

Bobby nodded. "Good. We leave at dawn. Meet me out at the freezer house."

"Something else we need to begin thinking about," I said. "We need more food, and more clothes. We need to think about a quick trip to Pine Valley."

Conversations buzzed then.

Finally, Susan spoke up. "Paul's right. We don't have enough to make it through the winter. We for sure need warm clothes, and any frozen food we can find. If we don't take it now, and the power goes out, the food will spoil. Now's the time for us to take advantage of what we can find."

There were several murmurs of agreement.

"Okay, we'll think about that for a day or two" I said. "Right now, let's worry about our search-and-destroy team, and the job they're going for tomorrow. Let's all say a silent prayer for them, and let's hope that they get the job done!"

Chapter 9

The group left at dawn the next morning. They took two flamethrowers and a two-gallon can of gasoline with them. They had a couple of other things that Bobby had shown me...two hand grenades he had liberated from the National Guard Armory.

The previous night, after the meeting, I had pulled Susan off to the side. Phyllis came, too.

"Susan, are you sure you want to do this?" I asked.

Susan looked at both of us, and saw the worry there. "Yes. I want to do this. For me, it's payback for losing Cheryl to those things."

"Is that all it is?" asked Phyllis.

Susan thought for a moment before answering. "Of course not. The world as we knew it is gone, and my life is gone, too, because Cheryl is gone. I don't plan to die on purpose, but let's just leave it at this: If I die, I won't mind. Is that what you wanted to know?"

With that speech, Susan walked away.

So, the next morning, the five of them left to hunt down the nest of the flying creatures. Before they left, I asked Bobby to come closer to me, and I whispered what little I knew about Manuel and Dr. Case's observations about him. Bobby said that he'd keep an eye on him.

They left with little fanfare, but a big crowd had turned out to see them for what most expected to be the last time. As they disappeared through the tree line, heading north, we all hoped for their success, and prayed silently for their safety.

Meanwhile, Phyllis and I talked to a few people about the plan to raid the town for more supplies. Strangely enough, Richie wanted to go. He even made a wise suggestion.

"Why don't we go at night? Most of the creatures are pretty dormant at night. It might be safer," Richie said.

I could have made a comment about the squirmers going dormant in the sunlight, but, instead, I leaned back in my chair and thought about it. It really was a good idea. "Richie, that's a great idea!"

The young man blushed a little, but seemed proud of the praise. Teresa was sitting next to him. She beamed at him, and linked her arm into his.

I looked at Phyllis. "Let's go tonight, then."

"If you think it's best, Paul," she replied.

"How much room is in the freezer?" I asked.

"Quite a bit," said Phyllis. "And if we fill it, there's always Susan's."

And that was that. We didn't talk about Susan or the others any more than that. We didn't expect them back for at least a day, and that was if they came back at all.

For tonight's raid, I would lead the way, and we'd take the bus. Billy Barnes would go, and Richie volunteered. Latisha was going, and wouldn't hear otherwise.

"You think you takin' my bus tonight without *me*?" she said. "You guess again, writer boy!"

Lee Adams, the elderly man from the RV, volunteered, and so did Bernice. I protested. I felt that they shouldn't come, but Bernice summed it up nicely.

"Paul, we can help. We're experienced with hardship, and you know we're dependable. What else are you looking for?"

Lee piped in with, "Yeah, and you know we'll stand our ground. We're too damn old to run."

I chuckled at his comment, and agreed that they could help.

Phyllis was worried. "Paul, don't you want a few more people to go with you? I'm afraid you don't have enough."

"No, honey, if we take more people, we won't have a lot of room in the bus. I think we'll be okay with what we have. We're only going to hit one grocery store and one clothing store. If we can find an undamaged Target or Wal-Mart, or something else that has both food and clothes, we'll just make one stop."

"Don't you want me to come with you?"

"Of course I do, but who would take care of the kids? We don't know when the others will be back, and, truthfully, I don't even know the names of most of these people. No, I want you to stay here with the children, and ask Dr. Case to stay alert, too."

Phyl didn't like it, but she didn't argue. It was logical.

We left at seven o'clock that night. It was well past sundown, and very little light was left in the sky.

Latisha drove. Everyone was fully armed with what we had, and Richie had strapped the flamethrower to his back. Latisha took her time going down the narrow road. It was an uneventful trip into Pine Valley.

"There's a Wal-Mart at the edge of town," Lee said. "We can give that a shot."

I nodded. "Let's do it. Would you please give Latisha directions?"

"Of course!" Lee moved up to stand next to Latisha, and within five minutes, we had pulled into the store's parking lot.

The parking lot had a few cars in it, but they looked abandoned. Some had doors standing wide open, and in some, the dome light still shone dimly. A couple of cars were overturned, and there was a huge dead millipede-looking creature underneath one of the overturned cars. It was dead...or, at least, we hoped it was dead. The lights in the store were still burning brightly, which meant that the freezers would still be operating. Latisha drove slowly past the front of the store. We saw no signs of people...or bugs.

"Where you want to park, Paul?" asked Latisha.

"Right in front of the door," I said. "And leave the engine running. If we have to make a fast exit, I don't want to wait for the engine to start."

Latisha brought the bus to a stop in front of the grocery side of the store.

I stood, and told everyone, "Okay, we're not looking for sizes in clothing. Take a shopping cart, and fill it up. Jeans, underwear, socks, shirts, and coats...all of that goes into your cart. When your cart is full, bring it out here and load it into the back. We are *not* splitting up! We stay together, and we all stay alert. Once we have our clothes, then we'll check out the groceries. Everyone ready?"

Everyone was.

"Okay, Richie, you'll use that flamethrower only as a last resort. We don't want to burn down the store before we've gotten what we need," I said.

Latisha opened the doors, and I led the way out of the bus. We gathered on the sidewalk in front of the entrance and listened. There wasn't a human sound to be heard. No talking, no dogs barking, no cars...nothing. That was bad.

On the other hand, we didn't hear any bug noises, either. That was good.

The first set of automatic doors slid open. We cautiously entered the building. We walked carefully through the vending machines, kids' ride 'em machines, and video kiosks. The second set of automatic doors slid open, and we entered the store itself. It was weird. There was no sound, no music coming across the speakers, and no people sounds. No 'boops' from the cash registers broke the silence, and no shopping carts could be heard rolling along the floor.

"Okay, I'm officially freaked out," said Billy. "I've never heard such total quiet in a store like this before."

"I know, right?" I said. "It's like the world has stopped." I took one last look around at what I could see of the store, and said, "Everybody get a shopping cart. Let's go get some clothes."

Pulling out the carts from the cart storage area seemed to make a huge noise. Each cart's rattling as it was pulled from the rest seemed to echo through the empty store, and coming back to us with a faint, hollow ring. Slowly, we pushed our carts through the store, pausing at every aisle intersection and looking all around us for any sign of movement.

"Have you noticed?" asked Bernice. "You would think the store would have been looted by now."

"Yeah. It's like nobody had time. The bugs must have hit hard and fast," replied Billy.

"Strange," I replied. "Let's just get ours and go."

We came to the clothing department. We started with ladies' clothing.

"Go with warm stuff, ya'll," said Latisha. "Sweatshirts first, bras, panties, jeans...oh! Paul, we got to get shoes, too!"

We began throwing clothing into buggies. We didn't worry about sizes or designs. We worried about warmth, and wearability. If it was for women, it went into a buggy.

We had just filled two of the shopping carts when we heard, "Hey! Stop that! Stop that right now!"

All six of us whirled to the sound of the voice, weapons raised and ready. Standing in the aisle, pointing his finger at us, was a skittish man with a tie. His name tag read "Walt – Assistant Manager" and his face had a comical look of surprise on it. His khaki pants suddenly had a dark spot that spread from his crotch to halfway to his knee. He had soiled himself from fear. Having five shotguns and a flamethrower pointed at you by surprised people might cause that to happen.

"Y-you people can't b-buh-be here," stammered Walt. "The company won't like it. And stealing is against the law!" His look of fear turned to a look of fear and hope. "There might be *charges!*" Walt said this last bit as if it mattered...as if it were the most important thing in his life.

I lowered my shotgun, and motioned for everyone else to lower theirs.

"Walt," I said. "My name is Paul Stiles. I have a cabin up in the mountains, and these people are staying with me. We need supplies, and we're taking these." I paused. "Walt, do you know about the bugs? The creatures?"

Walt had begun fumbling around in his pocket as soon as I had told him my name. By the time I finished talking, he had pulled out one of those 3x5 memo pads with the spiral wire holding the sheets of paper together. He then began fumbling in his pockets again.

"Need a pen, buddy?" asked Billy. He was holding one in his hand, his arm stretched out to Walt.

God forgive me, but Walt reminded me so much of Don Knotts at that moment, that it made me start laughing. I couldn't help it.

"What's funny, Paul?" asked Lee.

I quoted from the Andy Griffith Show. "Got your bullet, Barney?"

All of them except Richie understood the reference, and burst out laughing. Richie was too young, and had never watched the show.

Finally, I finished laughing. "So, Walt, you *do* know about the bugs, don't you?"

Walt, who had been scribbling, nodded. He put his arms to his sides, and burst out crying.

Bernice moved to the man's side, and put a hand on his shoulder. Walt responded to the touch by turning and burying his face on her shoulder. His crying intensified, and Bernice patted his back for several minutes, until he got himself under control. He finally pulled himself away from Bernice's shoulder, pulled out a handkerchief, and blew his nose loudly.

"Walt, you're coming back with us to my cabin." I turned to the rest of our group. "Right?"

Everyone made noises of agreement.

"Thank you." Walt gave one final wipe to his nose and tucked the cloth back into his pocket. "Yes, I know about the bugs. I killed one in the storeroom."

I know my mouth was open in astonishment. Billy eyed Walt with a new look, as if he were sizing him up. Richie had no expression, and Latisha nodded in understanding.

Lee was also amazed. "How did you do it, son?"

Walt smiled. "I mixed some boric acid with water in a five gallon gas can. Then, I climbed up on top of the shelves in the storeroom and waited for it to pass under me. I doused its head with it, and it died. Painfully." He paused. "It was one of those long things, like out in the parking lot."

A millipede creature. I was impressed with the simplicity. "How have you kept them out of the store?"

Walt's smile got even wider. "I sprayed an entire can of Raid at every entrance, and laid down some boric acid at the big doors in the back. I also pour some into each toilet after a flush."

"That is absolutely amazing." I turned to the others. "Can you believe how simple this is?"

"I use bleach sometimes, too," added Walt. "And pool chemicals. It all works, and it's kept them out so far."

I looked at Billy. He seemed to be as flabbergasted as I was. "I can't believe it's that easy."

Walt perked up. "Want to see the dead one? It's in the back!" He started walking toward the storage room in the back of the store.

"No, no, Walt, that's fine." I held my hand up to stop him. "Listen, Walt, we have a nice cabin up on the mountain, and we're taking you back with us. Is it just you?"

Walt shook his head. "No, there are two others here with me."

I nodded. "Good. Then they're coming, too. But, right now, we need to start loading supplies onto the bus, and now we're going to add a few things...like boric acid, bleach, and pool chemicals!"

Walt waved at the ceiling. A camera was there, behind its little darkened globe. Soon, another man and a young woman joined us.

Walt introduced them. The man was Carlton, and the woman was Heather.

"Pleased to meet you folks. Shall we all get started?" I began putting clothes into the carts again.

With nine people working, we soon had enough clothes, soap, camping gear, and chemicals. They filled half the bus. Now it was time to get the frozen stuff.

Latisha was ready to get moving. "I'm feelin' antsy, Paul. We need to get gone."

Billy agreed. "Yeah, I'm feelin' it too, Hoss."

I felt goosebumps along my arms. "So am I." I turned to Heather, who was standing with Richie. "Heather, there aren't any bugs here at night, are there?"

She shook her head. "Not usually, unless you count those moth-looking things. They chase the streetlights in the parking lot."

I felt cold inside. "How big are they?"

"About the size of a person's head. Not big at all, compared to some of the other bugs."

"Do they chase people?"

Again, Heather shook her head. "There haven't been any people around since those moth things showed up."

That told me exactly nothing. On one hand, the moth things could be harmless. On the other hand, they could be deadly to people.

I made an announcement to everyone. "Okay, everyone fill your carts with fresh meat. We can use some of that immediately, and freeze the rest. Then, pick up any frozen meat that will fit. I'll take a cart, and load it down with frozen vegetables. One cart apiece, and then let's hit the road. I got a bad feeling."

I believe everyone had a bad feeling, because we had all nine carts filled in ten minutes flat. We lined up at the door.

"Okay, just like before. Get the carts outside, and we'll start a bucket brigade for loading the bus. Let's go!" I led the way.

Outside, Billy and Richie fanned out slightly from us to keep watch. Lee, Bernice, and Latisha were inside the bus, putting the food away. Walt and I were outside the doors, passing the food inside. Carlton and Heather made up the rest of the bucket brigade. When we emptied a cart, we just pushed it out of the way and pulled the next one up.

Billy said quietly, "Incoming."

I turned to look, and from the north side of the parking lot, the moth creatures came. They came in a large swarm, and would swarm quickly over one of the lights in the parking lot. Then, a few would break off, and those few would swarm another light. And a few more would break off, and this third bunch would swarm over another light.

We had maybe thirty seconds before they were right over us.

"Walt, grab the cart! We'll lift it onto the bus and take it with us!" I lifted my side, Walt took the other, and we muscled that baby onto the bus. Latisha settled into the driver's seat, and Richie climbed aboard, too.

I was panicking. "Billy! Come *on!*"

Billy clambered aboard, and just as Latisha got the doors shut, we could hear the moth things peppering themselves against the sides of the bus.

"Reckon they harmless?" asked Latisha.

I was still in panic mode. "Who *cares?* Let's go!"

Latisha didn't need any further prodding. She stepped on the gas, and the bus pulled away from the front of the store. The big vehicle belched out a huge greyish-black cloud of exhaust. The exhaust fumes were apparently too much for the moth bugs to stand, because they didn't bother the bus again. They only did their swarming thing over the lights in the parking lot. A couple swooped down in front of the bus's headlights, but were smacked down into the pavement, and crushed under the big vehicle's wheels. The bus left the parking lot with the sound of screeching tires.

As we drove through the deserted streets of Pine Valley, we all began to relax a bit. It began to sink in that we had pulled off the supply raid. Walt, Carlton, and Heather had joined us, and we were on our way home.

"Paul." Latisha had spoken so quietly that I almost didn't hear her.

I moved up beside her. "What is it, Latisha?"

She waved one hand ahead of her. "I keep seeing things. It's like they're at the very edge of my headlights. But, when the light touches them, they duck out of sight."

"Bugs?"

Latisha nodded. "Yeah. It sure ain't people."

"You sure?"

She snorted. "They wayyy too big, Paul"

I turned to the others. "There are some big bugs dancing at the edge of our headlights. Other than the squirmers, what kind of bugs are nocturnal?"

"Lightning bugs!" called out Heather.

"Millipedes," said Walt.

"Mosquitos," said Richie.

"Spiders," added Carlton

I shuddered at spiders. Heaven help us if spiders mutants were in the mix.

"Moths, but we've already seen those," said Billy.

"What about ants? Do they come out at night?" asked Bernice.

"This is purely yucky, but Bernice and I know from living in Florida. Cockroaches," said Lee.

A cold chill ran down my back at that thought. Cockroaches bred so fast, and they would eat anything. They were almost impossible to kill, and scientists said that cockroaches would survive a nuclear holocaust.

And cold didn't bother them very much.

Surely those Russian scientists weren't dumb enough to use cockroaches, no matter how much the Islamic terrorists paid them. If they had, humanity surely was doomed.

Actually, the thought of ants was just as bad. Ants tunneled underground, and could lift many times their own weight. If ants had been genetically altered, there wouldn't be a safe place on earth.

I leaned over to Latisha. My voice was very low "Don't stop unless you have to. We've got to get out of here. Coming at night might not have been the best plan."

Latisha's voice was just as low. "Paul, we had to come, no matter *what* time it was. Food, clothes, other supplies...they wasn't just layin' around up there at the cabin."

I nodded. "I know."

Latisha's eyes widened. "Oh, *shit!*" She slammed on the brakes.

Ahead of us, crossing the road, was one of the millipede creatures. It was the size of a diesel locomotive. In its mouth was a cow. It was lowing pitifully, obviously in pain. The cow was probably the only reason the thing didn't come after us.

Everyone could see it, but the only sound came from Billy. "I don't think I'd want to go against that thing."

After the creature had passed us, Latisha slowly gained speed. We had no further bug incidents on the remainder of the trip home.

Chapter 10

When we arrived back at the cabin, Phyl was waiting on the porch for us. Dr. Case sat with her in the second rocking chair. Both were armed.

I introduced them to Walt, Heather, and Carlton, and we told them about our trip. By the time we finished our story, most of the remaining folks at the cabin had come around to listen. Only the children were still asleep. When I got to the part about the millipede creature and the cow, there were a couple of gasps, both at the fact that it was carrying a cow, but also at the size of the beast.

To be honest and fair with these people, we shared the part about things dancing just past the headlights, and our guesses as to what they were. I told them all about my fears of cockroaches and ants, and what could happen if DNA from those insects had been used by the Russian scientists.

One man in the back asked a question. "So you're saying that there's giant ants under us right now? Inside this mountain?"

I shook my head. "That isn't what I'm saying. I'm saying that if they exist, they could be. We're working in the blind here, people. We have no way of knowing for sure what has been used for DNA in any of these creatures."

The man continued his argument. "But, if that's the case, then they could come up under us any time! If that's true, they could come up and eat us any minute!"

"That's only a remote possibility! We don't know that they exist!"

The man was belligerent. "Well, just what the hell *do* you know, Mister?"

"Right now, you know everything that I know. Anything else is just speculation, and we have no facts to back them up. So let's not do any fear-mongering, shall we?" I wiped my forehead. "I just want everyone to know the facts. We haven't made any conclusions on any of it. It would be foolish to base anything on speculation of things we haven't seen."

The man fell silent, but I could see that his words had made an impression on some of the people there. The fear on their faces betrayed them.

"Let's just get the food unloaded, and get some sleep," I said. "It will be dawn soon. We can unload the rest during daylight."

Several, but not everyone, helped to unload the food. Others milled around, then slowly slipped away.

Phyllis told me that if we raided again, we'd have to begin storing food in Susan's freezer.

When I was alone with Phyllis, she wanted to talk.

"Paul, you frightened some of them tonight."

I nodded. "I know."

"Did you mean to?"

I thought for a moment. "Maybe not frighten, but make them aware of possibilities."

"I'm afraid those 'possibilities' might make some of them leave."

I looked into her eyes. "That might not be a bad thing, Phyl."

"Paul!"

"All along, I've said that if anyone doesn't want to play by my rules, they can leave. If they're too frightened to face the possibilities presented by these creatures, and they think they can do better somewhere else, then they're welcome to leave. I'll give them food and water for a few days, and I'll wish them luck...just like I wished Ben good luck." I took off my shirt and put it over the bedroom chair. "If they think they can find someplace better, or someone else that can lead them, I'd rather they leave. I don't want them sowing discontent or defeatism here."

"But is it the right thing to do?"

"I don't know. And I can't worry about it. I have to do what I feel is right for the group. I can't please everyone, no matter what choices I make."

AFTER THE SUN CAME up, I got up, too. Phyllis had gotten up already, and went downstairs to start breakfast for everyone. I hadn't been able to sleep very well, so I decided that I really needed a cup of coffee.

Teresa met me at the bottom of the stairs. "Phyllis needs to see you."

I nodded my thanks to the teen. "Kitchen?"

Teresa nodded.

I went into the kitchen and found Phyl and Bernice working at making breakfast.

"Hi, honey," I said. "Teresa said you were waiting for me."

"We lost about twenty people last night."

"What?"

Phyllis turned and looked at me. "I said we lost about twenty people last night. After you guys got home."

"Twenty?" I sat down heavily in one of the kitchen chairs.

Bernice tied up a trash bag. "Latisha said that they were mostly her passengers. Some kids, too."

Billy had just come into the kitchen with Lee. "They took a few weapons and some ammo with them. And food for a few days."

Lee looked at me, not wanting to ask the question that I had rolling around in my head. But, he asked it anyway. "Should we go after them?"

"No." I shook my head firmly. "This was their choice. This isn't a damn prison, and I'm not a damn guard. If someone decides that they want to go, then we'll all say a silent prayer for their safety, and move on."

Billy smiled lightly. "I'm glad to hear you say that, Paul. We were all afraid you'd want to do something foolish."

I shook my head again. "No, if they don't want to stay, we don't need them. As crass as it sounds, it'll make the food last longer."

Nothing more was said about the people that had left.

After breakfast, I put Teresa, Heather, Richie, Keith and Clarissa to work unloading the rest of the supplies we had brought home. While they unloaded, Richie had walked around to the front.

"Paul? You might want to come look at this."

I walked to the front of the bus. Embedded in the grill was one of the moth creatures. Its wings were still moving slightly.

"Richie, go get Dr. Case. Quickly, now."

Richie ran to the cabin and inside. Less than thirty seconds later, Dr. Case came running out of the front door, with Richie close behind him.

The good doctor skidded to a halt beside me. "Oh, this is great! It's still alive! Do we have something to put it in? I need to study this creature as much as possible, while it's still alive."

I snapped my fingers. "I have just the thing! Keith, Clarissa, come here."

Keith came over. I leaned over and whispered into his ear what I wanted and where it was. He ran into the cabin to get it. To Clarissa, I whispered what I wanted for her to bring, and she ran around to the back of the cabin with an enthusiastic grin.

The moth creature looked like it was part moth and part housefly. Its wings, from what we could see, was covered in the same kind of dust that moths have, but its body was compact, and shaped like a fly. Its tail was bluish-green, and we could see four legs. That was all we could see until we got it out of the bus grill.

Clarissa got back first, carrying a small piece of plywood and a pair of heavy work gloves.

As she handed me the two items, Keith tore out of the house with his assignment: a ten-gallon aquarium.

"Perfect! Thanks, kids!" Dr. Case was ecstatic.

I put on the gloves, and told Dr. Case what I wanted. "Now, I'm going to try to take this thing out as gently as I can. Once I have it out, I'll put it into the aquarium. Doc, you'll put the plywood over the top. Okay?"

The doctor had the plywood in his hands. He nodded. "Okay. I'm ready when you are, Paul."

The thing looked to weigh less than ten pounds. Its body was a little larger than a guinea pig. I reached over and took hold of the thing as gently as I could. It was really jammed into the grill, but with only a little maneuvering, I was able to pull it out. I heard the children gasp, and Teresa said, "Oh, man!" I put the creature into the aquarium, and Dr. Case put the plywood over the top.

I still hadn't seen the thing's face. But I had my chance then.

Its face was almost human. It had what looked like a human nose, and it looked broken. The 'nose' was bleeding, oozing black ichor. It had a slit under the nose, with fully-formed lips, and a slight chin. That's where the human resemblance ended, however. It opened and closed its mouth to breathe, and the mouth was full of tiny, sharp-looking teeth. Its tongue lolled out of its mouth, and the tongue was as long as its body, and was as black as night. It had two eyes set on either side of its broken nose, and they were milky and empty.

Two things hit me at once. These moth-creatures were fully-grown squirmers, and they had partial human DNA inside them!

It was the empty eyes that made me realize where these creatures originated.

I told Dr. Case my hypothesis.

"You may very well be right, Paul. It would explain why the infected people were still able to function after the eggs began hatching. The infected bodies recognized the human DNA. By the time the bodies realized that the larvae were dangerous, it was too late for the body to respond."

The creature suddenly began making a screeching, whining noise, and began fluttering its wings madly inside the aquarium, battering itself against the glass in an attempt to escape its prison.

Richie quickly placed a good-sized rock on top of the plywood. Hopefully, it would be heavy enough to keep the thing inside.

"Paul, will you help me carry this into your study?" asked Dr. Case.

"Will it be safe?"

Case studied the aquarium. "Yes, I think so. It won't be coming out of the fish tank alive."

I looked into the doctor's eyes. He nodded his assurance. I nodded my agreement, and we each picked up a side of the small, glass case. In no way was our prize heavy, but we didn't want our prisoner to flutter away if something happened to the plywood while only one person carried the container.

As we go to the cabin's porch, I called out to the kids. "Keith! Clarissa! Keep unloading the bus, please!"

The young people turned back to the bus and began unloading the chemicals and the clothing.

Phyllis met us at the door. "Paul Stiles, you are *not* bringing that thing into this cabin!"

"Phyllis, we have to. Dr. Case can give us answers."

"Dr. Case can get us all *killed!*"

"Phyllis, we're inside already. We're careful. And we'll keep the study door closed. It won't live long enough to kill anyone."

"How do you know that? A crystal ball?"

"Phyllis, *enough! Please!*"

Phyllis ran over to the kitchen, crying.

I stared daggers at Dr. Case. "This had better be worth it, Doc."

I had noticed something about our guest. Once inside, out of the sunlight, it had stopped fluttering and trying to escape. It settled quietly onto the bottom of its glass prison, and watched us carefully.

We set the aquarium down carefully onto the metal ambulance stretcher that Dr. Case was using as an examining table. Doc walked around to look at the thing's face.

"Incredible," he muttered to himself, barely audible. He turned to look at me. "Can you believe they used human DNA this way?"

"Yes, I can. And it sort of pisses me off."

Case looked a bit flustered. "Yes, me, too. But it *is* fascinating! How can this thing live? What does it eat? How does it reproduce? How do its eggs get inside a human body?"

"Some of those things we won't be finding out, will we, Doc?" I tried to keep my tone from sounding menacing, but I didn't particularly want to know this thing's mating habits.

Case smiled. "No, we won't be finding out how its eggs get inside human bodies. At least I hope we won't." He shrugged his shoulders. "If we do, it won't be from this guy, unless it comes from your gloves somehow."

I looked down. I still had them on. I quickly pulled them off, and left Dr. Case to his studies. I went to the kitchen and got a gallon-sized freezer bag, one with the yellow-and-blue stripes that turn green when the bag is sealed properly. I dropped the gloves inside, sealed the bag, and washed my hands thoroughly. The freezer bag went into the kitchen trash, which I then took outside to the burn barrel. I went back inside and washed my hands again.

Paranoia is a great motivator.

Now I had to swallow my own paranoia and find Phyllis, so that I could convince her that her paranoia wasn't something to worry about.

Chapter 11

An hour or so later, with my ears still ringing and chilly from the cold ass-chewing delivered to me by my sweet wife, I heard Keith again calling from the front yard.

"Dad! Dad! C'mere! *Daaadd!*"

I ran outside to see what was the matter.

Keith saw me. He pointed and shouted, "Look!"

I looked in the direction that he pointed. What I saw shocked me.

Manuel, Susan, Michael, and Bobby were coming out of the trees. Bobby held a rope. Tied to that rope, and being dragged behind him, was one of the flying creatures that they had gone after. It was dragged headfirst, and the rope was tied in an elaborate harness. Its wings were duct-taped to its body. It, too, had milky, empty eyes. But, even with empty eyes, it gave off an almost overpowering feeling of anger...at us.

I looked around. "Welcome back! And I see you brought a visitor!" I looked toward the trees. "Bobby, where's Nick?"

Bobby shook his head once. "Long story. We'll tell everyone everything later. We're all exhausted. Where's Dr. Case?"

"Keith, go get Dr. Case! Hurry!" I said to my son.

"We found the nest. It's gone. This is the sole survivor, as far as we could tell," huffed an exhausted Michael.

"Alive, just like Dr. Case ordered," added Susan.

Manuel mumbled something in Spanish, ending with the word, *muerte.*

Death.

On that cheerful note, Dr. Case burst through the front door of the cabin. He came to a stop within two feet of Bobby's big game trophy. His voice could barely be heard.

"Oh, my God."

"Listen, Doc, don't get too close to the ass end of that thing. Trust me on that. It's not *just* a stinger." Michael's face showed distaste.

"What do you mean?" asked the doctor.

Bobby sighed. "It's also a reproductive organ. We saw it with Tyrese, and with Pablo. These things had laid eggs in them. The eggs hatched, and both men were still alive."

At that point, the creature screamed. Again, like the one that screamed in the front yard during the bug attack, it was loud and very high-pitched. Its single antenna vibrated with the scream, and its snout was opened wide. After a few seconds, the scream faded.

"Oh, yeah," said Susan. "We forgot to tell you that it does that every so often. Like it's calling for help."

I looked at her. "And you guys wiped out its nest? And everything alive inside it?"

Susan nodded. "We did."

Bobby was almost to the point of collapsing. "I'm hoping there aren't any others." He handed me the rope. "I'm going to lie down on something soft, and sleep for a day or two. You're welcome, Dr. Case."

Dr. Case perked up, remembered his manners, and said, "Oh! Yes! Thank you, Bobby!"

After Bobby and the rest of his team went into the cabin, I handed the rope to Dr. Case. "Here you go, Doc. This one does *not* come inside the cabin!"

THAT EVENING, EVERYONE gathered outside, under the stars. The temperature was comfortable, in the mid-fifties, so it wasn't too cold to enjoy the night. Everyone had jackets or extra shirts on, so the clothing raid was a success.

The rocking chairs and porch steps were reserved for the four members of the search-and-destroy team. Everyone wanted to hear the story, so, after dinner, we all gathered around.

Bobby started. "There are two things I should mention before we tell this story. One is that we didn't see any form of natural wildlife at all, except for a few birds. So, unless these creatures can be safely eaten as meat, we're in trouble in that respect. Second, those wasp-things aren't the only bugs in these mountains."

There was a collective gasp at that remark. Dr. Case didn't seem surprised, and I had suspected it.

Bobby continued. "I have a theory about that. If I'm not mistaken, most of these creatures are warm-blooded, and have lungs."

Dr. Case nodded his agreement.

"Dr. Case agrees. So, if these things are warm-blooded, and have lungs...well, the mountains aren't as safe as we were told." There were murmurs around the crowd. Bobby held up a hand. "It's not so surprising. We call these things 'bugs', but they have DNA from other animals, too...even humans."

Murmurs of agreement went through the crowd. Most of them had seen the moth-creature at some point during the day.

Bobby looked at me, and then glanced around the crowd. "We started out that, and had gone about a mile, when we came to a huge hill of dirt. There was an opening at the top of the hill, but we didn't venture close enough to see what was inside. We had seen one of its residents going into the hole, and we didn't want any part of them."

Manuel looked very frightened. "They were mostly *ants*! Big, ugly-looking things!"

Bobby nodded. "They did seem to have more ant parts to them more than anything else. We left that alone, because we weren't looking for them. We can save a raid on them for another day.

"We snuck past the anthill, or whatever it was, and kept going. We had to hide twice more within another mile, both times to hide from huge millipede creatures. One was carrying a dead pig."

I interrupted Bobby long enough to tell him about the millipede in Pine Valley that had been carrying a cow.

Bobby nodded. "They seem to be dangerous, but they aren't fast moving. We were able to evade one that chased us. We just ran, and it couldn't keep up.

"By the time we had put five miles behind us, we heard the buzzing well before we saw the nest. The wasp-creatures had found a natural cave to use as their nest."

Keith spoke up. "I know that cave! Remember, Dad? We all hiked to it last year!"

I smiled and nodded. "I remember."

Bobby smiled. "I'm glad you know the place. Nick volunteered to ease up to the entrance, to see what we could do about it. He had just peeked inside when one of the creatures – maybe it was a sentry – came out of the cave. It pounced on him, held on with its claws, and punctured his body several times with its stinger thing. Then it carried him inside the nest, and Nick was screaming all the while." Bobby wiped his forehead with his hand. "Suddenly, the screaming stopped, right in the middle of a scream. We never knew what had happened to him, but we knew he was gone for good."

Bobby took a sip of coffee from the cup he was holding.

Susan picked up the story. "We sort of fell apart when Nick was pulled into the nest. I wanted to bull my way in there, and start shooting every one of them. Manuel held me back, bless him...because what we did was brilliant.

"We had noticed that the rocks above the cave looked looser than they should have been, so Bobby came up with a plan."

Michael added, "It was brilliant the way it worked."

Manuel nodded. "*Si*. Michael and I moved around until we were in throwing distance of the rocks. Bobby and Susan moved so that they could cover the entrance with the flame throwers."

I could see what they had planned, and so could several others. I smiled to myself, because it was a beautiful plan.

Susan laughed. "When Bobby and I opened up on the entrance with the flamethrowers to keep the creatures inside, Manuel and Michael each threw a grenade at the rocks above the entrance. When the grenades exploded, the rocks closed off the cave, and the wasps were trapped inside."

"Our P.O.W. was outside the cave when we attacked, and tried to get inside. A loose boulder rolled down the hill and smacked it directly on the head," added Bobby. "Knocked the bastard unconscious. We taped and tied that sucker up as fast as we could. Otherwise, Dr. Case wouldn't have had his specimen."

As if on cue, the wasp-creature screamed again.

Bobby shook his head. "That thing has been doing that ever since it woke up!"

"Are you absolutely sure that those things can't get out of the cave?" I asked.

"Unless there's another way out, or if those things are stronger than I thought, I don't see how they could," answered Bobby.

I was thinking to myself. Maybe the wasp-creatures weren't strong enough...but what if the ant-creatures that the team saw were? Could two species of these things work together? And could they communicate with each other? I needed to get Bobby, Michael, and Dr. Case alone, and talk this over with them.

That pretty much ended the group meeting. It wasn't as big a group as it was previously, but still a good-sized group.

Bobby came up to Phyl and I, and actually asked about it. "Did some of the group leave?"

Phyllis answered him. "Yes. About twenty people left, right after Paul got back from the raid on Pine Valley. They just crept away in the night."

I added, "And we may lose a few more, since you spoke about that anthill. That, and the fact that other bugs are in the mountains."

Bobby shook his head. "I hate to see them go, but we may be better off without them."

"You, too?" said Phyllis. "That's almost exactly what Paul said!"

Bobby shrugged. "Hey, they might have the right idea. Moving around may be better than staying in one place. We just don't know yet."

I kept my voice low. "Hey, I'd like to talk to you and Michael. Think you guys can meet me in Dr. Case's room in about ten?"

Bobby nodded. "Sure. Let me round up Michael."

I told Phyl that I'd be up to bed later, and went to find Dr. Case.

THE FOUR OF US WERE in my former study. The moth-thing was staring at us with its empty eyes.

I started the discussion. "I have a couple of things that I want...no, *need* to know, and I want input from all of you."

Everyone nodded.

"Something occurred to me during the team's story, and I need some speculation. Can these different species communicate with each other? Can they work together? What have you found out, Jeremiah?"

Dr. Case crossed his arms and thought about it for a minute. "I've noticed that since the team brought back the wasp-creature, this little fella has calmed down considerably." He tapped the plywood on top of the aquarium. "It's possible, I suppose." He nodded, mostly to himself. "Probably quite likely. I don't know of any instances of any of the bugs attacking each other." He looked up at us. "So, if I had to guess, I'd say yes, they can communicate."

"Oh, shit," said Michael.

"Not good," agreed Bobby.

I stood up. "We need to kill both of these creatures now, before they can tell anything else where we are."

Michael stood up. "If they haven't already."

Dr. Case nodded. "Okay. I'll take care of this one. I would guess that a bullet in the head would take care of the other one."

"I'm on it," said Bobby.

"I'll come with," I said. "Michael, do you want to help the doc?"

"Sure."

"Good. Bobby and I will be back in just a minute."

As Bobby and I left the room, Dr. Case was opening his chloroform bottle, and getting a cloth ready.

When we got outside, the wasp-thing screamed again.

"It almost has to be calling the troops," I said. "And, if it is, we're in big trouble."

Bobby jacked a shotgun shell into the chamber as we walked. "We probably already are in big trouble, Paulie."

The creature was behind the cabin, left out in the open. As we walked up, Bobby aimed his gun at the thing's head, and pulled the trigger. The things head exploded, and it's body relaxed. It was dead, as near as we could tell. Bobby jacked another shell into the shotgun's chamber, and this time delivered the shot into the thing's chest. The chest also exploded.

"That should do it," he said, calmly turning and walking back to the cabin.

I followed behind my cop friend, wallowing in my own deep thoughts. I didn't notice until we stopped that Bobby didn't go back into the cabin. He had stopped beside the gasoline tanker, and picked up one of the five-gallon cans we kept full.

Understanding that we were about to burn the creature, I picked up a second can and followed.

Bobby doused the creature liberally with almost the entire can, set it down, and pulled out a pack of matches. The creature ignited with a loud "FWOOMP", and we settled in to watch it burn.

"Paul, I can watch this, if you'll go inside and get the other one. We need to burn it, too."

"Good idea. I'll be right back."

As I entered the cabin, I met Michael and Dr. Case. They were carrying the aquarium. The moth-thing looked dead, and I said as much.

"Dead as a doornail," said Michael. "We were bringing it outside. We didn't want to leave it in there."

"Good," I replied. "Take it around back. We're burning the big one, and we're going to burn this one, too."

When we got to the back, the big creature was still burning. I took the plywood off of the aquarium, and tossed it into the fire. Dr. Case tossed the moth-creature into the fire, aquarium and all.

The good doctor was quite serious when he said, "Let that be the end of it for a while."

We could only pray that his request was heard.

THE NEXT MORNING, AFTER breakfast, Richie ran into the cabin to get me.

"Paul! You gotta come! Billy heard something on the gas truck's CB radio!"

I'm sure that my eyes were as wide as saucers as I ran outside with Richie and over to the cab of the gasoline truck. Bobby was already there, and so was Michael.

"Is it true?" I asked breathlessly.

Bobby was grinning ear to ear. "Check it out for yourself!" He flipped a thumb back to the cab of the truck.

Billy was sitting inside the truck, listening to the broadcast. "I tried to respond, but we're apparently too far away from them. This radio doesn't have enough power to reach them. They must be boosting their power somehow."

The radio jumped to life. "This is Fort Simon Air Force Base. We are located twenty miles northwest of Pine Valley. All civilians are welcome here, if you can make it safely. The bugs are in control of most of the world, but we are secure here, with food, water, and shelter."

There was a pause, then the broadcast began again. There were variations in the wording, so we knew that it wasn't a recording.

The voice on the radio began speaking again. "Hi! Great to hear from you! What's your position?"

"They're talking to someone!" said Billy.

"Hey, that's great! Sure, we have room. Our scouts have reported that there are a few millipede creatures between you and the base, but you should be able to avoid them easily."

We listened to the silence, then the voice came back.

"We could send out an escort if you'd like. We have teams of four volunteers each that are sent out each time we contact a new group. They'll escort you in, and help fend off any bug attacks."

Silence again.

When the voice came again, there was laughter in the speaker's voice. "I'm Sergeant Hayes, sir. I'll be glad to meet you, too. We'll send a team to you at that location, and they'll bring you here to safety. I'm going to ask you to switch to another channel, channel thirteen, so that we can continue broadcasting on this one. Good luck!"

Silence, and then Sergeant Hayes began the broadcast we had heard earlier.

Billy turned the radio off. We were all quiet for a moment.

I broke the silence. "Wow. Twenty miles, but bugs."

Bobby agreed. "Yeah. Bugs."

I sighed. "Okay, meeting time, I guess. Everyone needs to know about the army base, and I guess we can vote on whether to go or not." I looked at them. "Do you guys mind helping me notify everyone? We'll meet in the front yard."

Everyone agreed, and set off to notify our group of survivors.

TWENTY MINUTES LATER, everyone in our group knew everything that we knew.

One man in the back of the group said, "So you're saying that we should go to this Air Force Base?"

I shook my head. "No. I'm only saying what we heard on the radio. On something this big, we vote on what to do."

A woman standing beside him said, "What do you think we should do, Paul?"

"It's Brittany, right?" The woman nodded. "Brittany, I don't have a clue." Everyone chuckled a bit at that, but it was mostly nervous chuckling. "Here, we have food, shelter, and some defenses. At Fort Simon, Sergeant Hayes said that they had those things, too. I'm sure that their defenses are stronger than ours, but, get too many people together in one place in a situation like this, and it's hard to defend everyone. You're more likely to be a casualty while you're waiting for someone to tell you what to do." I shrugged. "The choice has to be made by the group this time. It would be a long, dangerous trip through the mountains, and God only knows what we'll find along the way."

There was some low murmuring through the group. Michael stood up, and waved his hands for attention.

"I just want to say one thing, folks. Keep in mind, we've been damned lucky so far, if you stop and think about it. Of those of us that have stayed, we've only lost a few people to bugs...and that's saying a lot, considering the rest of the world! Sure, a few people have left our group, and I pray constantly that they've made it to safety. Personally, I would rather stay here, but I'll go where the group votes to go." Michael abruptly turned and sat down. His face was bright red.

Someone yelled, "What do you think, Bobby?"

Bobby stood and looked around slowly at everyone. You could have heard a pin drop. "I think we should go."

The crowd began talking, with some saying, "Really?", and others saying "You're kidding!" Bobby raised his hands for quiet, and the crowd quieted down.

"We're sitting ducks here," continued Bobby. "We have good defenses, but the bugs will find us sooner or later. When they do, can we hold up against a sustained attack from them? Sure, we can burn them, but what else do we have? What else can we use?"

Walt raised his hand. "We have chemicals. Boric acid. Bug spray."

Bobby nodded. "Yes, we do, Walt. But we don't have a lot of any of that. Our food may last until spring, but what do we do after that?"

Uncomfortable murmurs could be heard throughout the crowd.

"I don't think the bugs will let us plant any crops to amount to anything, do you?"

Cries of "No!" could be heard.

"But...if we're among a group of soldiers, and we all do our part and keep a good guard around, we might be able to plant and survive at Fort Simon." Bobby started back to his seat, then stopped and faced the crowd. "That's my thinking, anyway." He sat down.

"Do we want to discuss this all day?" I asked the group. "I mean, we can, if that's what you want to do. But I strongly recommend that we vote, so that we can start planning, whatever the vote may be. You all know what we know, so it boils down to speculation. Do we take a chance and head for Fort Simon, or do we take a chance and stay here through the winter?"

Most of the group just looked around at each other. Phyllis looked at me, asking me with her eyes what I wanted to do, and I shrugged. I didn't know. When Phyllis shrugged, I knew that we would stay here, regardless of how the vote turned out.

I turned to Michael and Bobby, and asked them to help me keep count of the vote. Both nodded and stood.

I raised my hands to quiet the group. "Okay, it's time to vote. Raise your hand as I ask each question." Several people nodded their understanding. "Okay, those of you who think we should...*HOLY SHIT!*"

The chainsaw noise was fast and loud as the sky over the yard was filled with wasp-creatures. At the same time, millipede-creatures burst through the treeline with a determined pace. Directly behind them came several ant-looking creatures, picking up trees and throwing them several feet away from them as they scrambled toward our group. Flying alongside the wasp-creatures were about fifty of the same kind of bugs that we had seen in the grocery store back in the city. Each one still had that long, sharp proboscis, and the single antenna between their black, empty eyes.

The bugs had caught us all off-guard.

And they were working together.

"The children!" I shouted. "Phyllis, get the children inside the milk truck and shut the door!" She gathered up the five children still with our group, and hustled them toward the milk truck.

I didn't have to tell anyone to start shooting at the bugs. They were shooting anything that flew, or was larger than themselves. But, the surprise was complete – many of us didn't have our weapons in our hands when the bugs came, and we wasted precious seconds picking them up, switching off safeties, and making sure that they were fully loaded.

"Flamethrowers! Get the flamethrowers!" I shouted. "Billy! Get to the gas truck! Fill the moat!"

Billy heard and ran in that direction. Before he had taken five steps, an ant-thing got him. It snagged him in its pincers, and snapped him in two. As Billy died, he fired his shotgun into the thing's head, and the ant-thing died along with him.

I counted ten of the millipede-creatures. Seven of them had people in their mouths, and were carrying them away, back into the treeline. They had armor, much like an armadillo, and bullets didn't seem to penetrate it.

Richie had decided to take over for Billy, and made a run for the gas truck. He made it. We had rigged a sort of filler pipe that ran from the place that normally would hold the hose used to put the gasoline into underground tanks at your local gas station, to the moat we had built. All that had to be done was to flip the trip switch, and the gasoline would flow through the feeder pipe into the moat. Richie began filling the moat. He was dodging fly-creatures as he waited, shooting one every so often. The wasp-creatures couldn't get to him, because the bus was parked very close to the gas truck. The big fliers couldn't get between the two vehicles to get to Richie.

Someone had brought out the three flamethrowers, and had given one to Michael. He strapped it on, and aimed it at one of the wasp-things. It soon was enveloped in flames, and had some of the fly-creatures following it as it crashed into the ground, screaming and burning. I could hear other screaming, and I hoped that it was from the mouths of bugs as they died, and not from any of our people.

To my horror, I could see an ant-thing trying to topple the milk truck. As I watched, I tried to aim at the bug, but someone jostled me as I pulled the trigger, and the shot went wild. A second ant-thing appeared beside the first, and the two of them were able to first rock the truck, then topple it over onto its side. I only hoped that Phyllis and the children weren't hurt inside the solid compartment on the back of the truck.

Michael saw the ant-things then, and turned the flamethrower on them. They immediately screamed and made a mad dash back into the trees surrounding the property. Some of the underbrush caught on fire, but I didn't care.

Several people were on the ground, with fly-things feeding from their body fluids. Each fly-thing's proboscis was jammed into the person's body, and looked like half-inch-wide tubes inserted into each person. The fly-things must have been part mosquito, because they would literally gorge themselves on whatever fluids they could drain. Most of the people they had landed on were not moving, and the creatures were very sluggish once they had their fill. They couldn't fly very well, and were dispatched quickly. The people were not so lucky.

Richie had to run away from the gas truck, because some of the ant-things were crawling under the truck to get to him. As he ran, a flaming wasp-creature crashed into the moat on the opposite side of the property, and the moat flamed up quickly. It caught four of the millipede-things, and caused them to burn. Ant-creatures were cut off from escaping, and we began executing them quickly. Several of the fly-things and wasp-creatures were also engulfed by flames as the fire spread along the moat. Two of them crashed into the cabin, and it was soon burning merrily.

The moat worked beautifully, except for one small problem.

Richie had not been able to shut off the gas flow from the truck before he got away from it.

The flame found the path to the overflow pipe, and quickly traveled up to the truck itself. Adding to the madness, the truck exploded with a huge fireball that engulfed all of the other vehicles that were parked nearby. The only surviving vehicle was the milk truck, and it was on its side.

The concussion from the blast knocked down most of the surviving people in our group, and caused the bugs to retreat...those that *could* retreat, anyway.

Now, every building on the property was burning, and the front yard was littered with dead and dying people...and bugs. We had to get out of there, and quickly.

I ran to the milk truck, and pried open the door to the back. Phyllis and the children all crawled out. Bobby came from nowhere, and helped me get them all to their feet. They were all bruised, but nothing was broken.

Susan, running up to us, said, "We have to retreat to my cabin! Let's *go!*" She had a cut on her head that had bled, and the blood covered half of her face. "The fire is dying along the moat! We can jump across! Come *on!*"

We followed her, along with what few survivors were left.

There weren't many.

Phyllis and I, Bobby, Susan, Latisha, Richie, Walt, Teresa, Michael, Millie, Dr. Jeremiah Case, Heather, and the five children – Keith, Clarissa, Zach, Martin, and Emily. Seventeen people. We were all that was left.

Chapter 12

That's almost the end of our story.

We crossed the moat, each of us assisting one of the children in jumping across, and we made the climb up the mountain to Susan's cabin. There was very little talk among us as we climbed, and, once we got to the cabin, we all just sat and stared at nothing. We all had minor cuts, bruises, and burns.

Jeremiah diagnosed us all as being in shock.

Duh.

The only clothes we had were the ones we had on, and the only weapons we had were the ones we carried.

We had food, of course. I told you that Susan's cabin was set up much like ours, with windmills, solar panels, and an outdoor walk-in freezer.

No, food wasn't the problem.

Our hope had been taken.

The tiny bit of hope we had all managed to cling to had been blown away by the bug attack, and gone up in the smoke of the inferno. We had foolishly thought that we were secure, and could survive anything.

But, the bugs had other ideas, and had crushed us as easily as we might...well...squash a bug.

Bobby, Michael, and I decided the next day to go back down the mountain and see if there was anything we could salvage. The smoke, which could be seen all that previous day rising through the trees, had dissipated to a small, black stream. Susan chose to go with us, and so did Latisha.

"Ya'll ain't goin' nowhere without me," scolded Latisha.

We left Walt and Richie on guard, and we cautiously went down the mountain.

The cabin was the thing that was still smoking. The wood had burned quickly, and a blackened mess on a concrete foundation was all that was left of our dream vacation home. All of the vehicles were burned-out husks, including Susan's, which had been brought down a few days earlier. Cheryl's car was still at Susan's cabin, but was filled with dead squirmers and dead moth-creatures. It was unusable.

The solar cells had been knocked to the ground. The generator building was burned to the ground, and the equipment inside was scattered, as were the batteries. The windmills were toppled. The well house had burned, and the plastic that surrounded the filter on the top of the well had melted, and covered the top. We could probably open the well, and use the water, but why would we? There was no shelter left. Everything had burned when the gas truck exploded.

The bodies of the people that had died were gone, and so were the dead bugs.

I offered the suggestion that they had all been taken by the ant-creatures, to be used as food, since that's what ants did. No one commented.

There were some weapons that we salvaged, and a little bit of ammo. Sitting in the middle of the front yard, undamaged and with no reason to be there, was the box containing the flare gun and the flares. Amazingly, it had survived both the explosion and the fires. We took it.

There were a few clothing items scattered around, and we took them, too.

We also took some of the frozen food that was scattered around. There wasn't much that hadn't either burned or thawed out in the sun, but we took what little we could find.

After we had gathered what we could, and made sure that no one was left to be buried, we once again climbed the mountain to Susan's cabin.

We stowed away what little we had salvaged, and told the others what we had seen. And that was that.

PER DR. CASE'S ORDERS, we took it easy for the next week. We needed to heal, and rest up.

We're leaving, you see.

We've decided that we can't stay here. We all think that it would be a huge mistake. It would only be a matter of time before the bugs found us again, and attacked. We might survive, but we might not. We have less to work with here at Susan's cabin, because most of the defensive supplies were at the other cabin. The gasoline is gone, except for what little is stored to operate the generators, so, without that, the moat is pretty much useless.

We lost the boric acid and the other insect chemicals in the explosion and the fire.

All we have left are our weapons – a few shotguns, a couple of handguns, and two flamethrowers that are almost out of fuel. Susan has a garden sprayer – one of those that must be pumped up by hand to have any pressure. We've filled that with gasoline, and we can use it along with the flare gun if we have to set a bug on fire when the flamethrowers run out of fuel.

We've kept a running guard twenty-four hours a day, and we've all taken shifts. Michael spotted a millipede-thing through the trees three days ago, and, last night, Richie fired some shots and brought down two moth-creatures. We were surprised to see them this high up the mountain, but there they were.

The cold isn't holding the bugs off. They're definitely warm-blooded, and they're growing larger. The moth-creatures that that Richie shot down were the size of Labrador retrievers.

I've spent the last week using up all of Susan's composition books to write down what has happened. It's a chore, writing in longhand...but it's been very therapeutic, too.

We're leaving tomorrow morning, heading northwest toward Fort Simon. We'll be going on foot, since vehicles are no longer an option. We'll have to cross two mountains and three long valleys before we get there. It will be a long hike.

Winter is coming, and the nights will be cold. And we don't know what waits for us along our trek. We may die between here and there, but that's a chance we're all willing to take.

Because the bugs know we're here.

I'll leave these notebooks on the dining table here in Susan's cabin. Maybe, someday, I can retrieve them. Or, maybe someone else will come along, find them, and gain some hope from our experiences.

Because hope is the only thing that separates us from the bugs with the empty eyes.

About The Author: T. M. Bilderback is a former radio announcer with a number of story ideas running around inside his head, most based on, or inspired by, classic songs. The author currently resides in Tennessee, and is writing feverishly in order to banish these stories from his head and into book form, before they drive him screaming into the street.

Other works by T. M. Bilderback

Nicholas Turner

If You Could Read My Mind

Justice Security

Mama Told Me Not To Come

Someone Saved My Life Tonight

Jackie Blue

Wake Me Up Before You Go-Go

Saturday In The Park

MacArthur Park

The Little Drummer Boy

The Night Chicago Died

Jim Dandy

Cow Patty

Hell's Bells

Tales Of Sardis County

Don't Come Around Here No More

Junior's Farm

The Devil's In The Details

I'm Your Boogie Man

Colonel Abernathy's Tales

The Lion Sleeps Tonight

Heart Of Glass

Other Stories

The Wreck Of The Edmund Fitzgerald

Gold

Hot Child In The City

Eli's Coming

Other Novels

Empty Eyes

Story Collections

Greatest Hits

Don't miss out!

Visit the website below and you can sign up to receive emails whenever T. M. Bilderback publishes a new book. There's no charge and no obligation.

https://books2read.com/r/B-A-KAW-YUIY

BOOKS 2 READ

Connecting independent readers to independent writers.